GHOSTS
of
BABYLON

A Novel

by

R.A. MATHIS

ISBN: 1478130091
ISBN 13: 9781478130093

Library of Congress Control Number: 2012911543
CreateSpace, North Charleston, SC

This book is dedicated to all those who serve our country. It is also dedicated to the families who have waited patiently, prayed ceaselessly, and cried countless tears for their loved ones in harm's way. Let us always honor their sacrifices, for they are made on our behalf.

Acknowledgements

I owe a debt of gratitude to those who helped to bring this book to life. Readers Cindy Vassar, Kim Moore, Bill & Patsy Williams, Claire Crouch, Steve Eldridge, and Dr. Robert L. Williams of the University of Tennessee helped with their comments, questions, and recommendations. And thank you, Sue Townsend, for motivating me to "put pen to paper."

Thanks to Russell Lee Klika for generously granting permission to use of the cover photo (which he took during our Iraq deployment).

Special thanks to Carolyn Boling who worked long and hard to convince me to clean up my prose and trust readers to understand nuances that didn't need explanations. Thanks also to her husband, Dr. Edward Boling, for his patience while she spent so much time on this project.

Thanks also to Frank Weimann for his help, suggestions, and belief in the project as well as Elyse Tanzillo for her kindness, patience, and professionalism.

This book would still be a work in progress if not for my story consultant, writing coach, and developmental editor Jay Wurts. Words cannot express my appreciation for his tireless efforts in getting this manuscript ready for publication and instructing me in the writer's craft.

To my copy editor, Emily Ball, thank you for beating the bushes and chasing the bugs (that I put there) out of the manuscript.

Thank you to my parents and brother for their love, support and help both in Iraq and at home and living what they teach – God and family always come first.

Most of all, I am eternally grateful the support my loving wife, Missy, and our three children who wait patiently, pray ceaselessly, and love unconditionally in both war and peace, good times and bad. I love and treasure you all more than words can say.

IRAQ

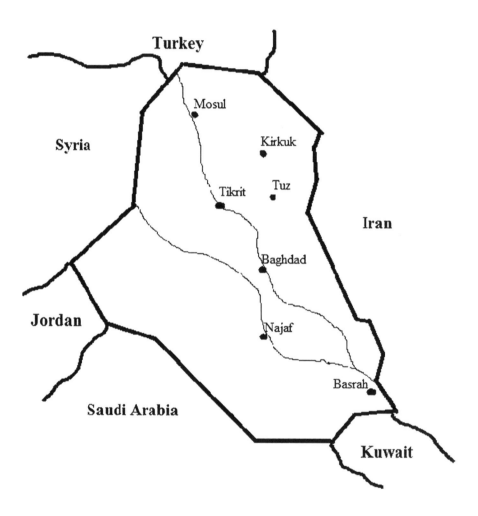

Turkey

Syria

Mosul

Kirkuk

Tikrit

Tuz

Iran

Baghdad

Jordan

Najaf

Saudi Arabia

Basrah

Kuwait

MAP OF TUZ AREA OF OPERATIONS

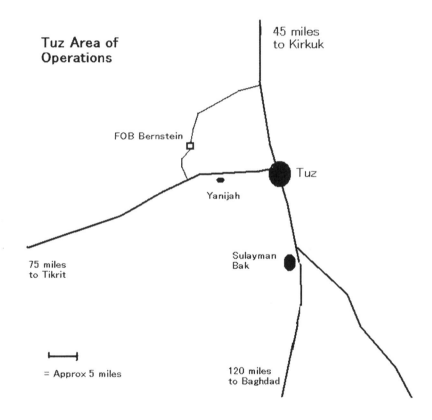

Tuz Area of Operations

45 miles to Kirkuk

FOB Bernstein

Tuz

Yanijah

75 miles to Tikrit

Sulayman Bak

= Approx 5 miles

120 miles to Baghdad

He who battles monsters take care
lest he become a monster
and if you gaze long into the abyss
the abyss gazes into you.

- Friedrich Nietzsche

INTO THE ABYSS

Northeastern Iraq
Spring 2005

Nobody really believes in Hell – until they get there. Stuart was a believer now, cowering behind a boulder as bullets ricocheted all around him. The arid, craggy landscape echoed the sounds of war like a primeval conductor directing a chaotic symphony of death. A round impacted the rock inches from Stuart's head, peppering his face with gravel and grit.

It seemed like half of Iraq was trying to kill him. Stuart expected death to come any moment. *So this is how it ends.* Knowing he'd volunteered to come here made it even worse. *What the hell was I thinking? I'm an archaeologist, not a soldier.* The benign lecture hall and comfy bed he left only two weeks ago seemed like another lifetime.

An Iraqi boy clung to Stuart for protection. Clutching the boy tightly, he thought of his own daughter and wished he could see her just once more. Not that he'd ever been much of a father to her. Chalk up one more regret.

An attacker darted into their refuge. He was so close Stuart could smell his sweat. The rank assailant raised his assault rifle with a savage grin. Stuart shielded the boy with his own body and closed his eyes. A shot rang out. No pain. Stuart opened his eyes. The intruder was dead. *But who shot him?* More shots. Two more foes went down.

Stuart turned to see an Army captain gripping a smoking pistol. The soldier produced another handgun, pressed it into Stuart's hand and said, "Make every shot count." He pointed to a Humvee sitting a few hundred feet away. It looked like miles to Stuart. The captain shouted, "Let's go!"

Stuart grabbed the boy's hand and the three of them bolted toward to vehicle. The captain went down after a few steps. Stuart sent the child on and rushed to help the fallen soldier.

He dragged the wounded man a short distance before a searing pain shot through his leg. The limb collapsed. He crashed to the ground.

Stuart sat up and examined his leg. A jagged shard of bone protruded from a gaping wound in his thigh, but he felt no pain. He didn't feel much of anything. The cracks of the guns and the screams of the men around him were muffled and distant. He looked up at the chaotic scene. None of it seemed real. Just a terrible nightmare.

There was a noise in the sky. He looked up, but saw nothing. The air crackled as if filled with invisible lightning. The hair on Stuart's neck stood on end. Someone yelled, "Incoming!"

Then the world exploded in a maelstrom of fire and steel.

1

Two Weeks Earlier
The University of Tennessee
Knoxville, Tennessee

"Politics and religion. Two sides, same coin."

Dr. Stuart Knight, hands clasped behind his back, paced the aisle of the packed lecture hall like a tweedy cop on a familiar beat. "Archaeologists are often caught between these forces. *Politics* is another word for corruption. And don't get me started on religion! Why must humans always prove that our imaginary friends are better than our neighbors?"

The class chuckled, but a few disapproving glares told Stuart he had hit the mark.

Good. He smiled. *The truth is supposed to hurt!*

"Case in point: Iraq, formerly known as Mesopotamia. The cradle of our civilization. Home to the earliest known settlements in the Western world. Politics and religion have kept archaeologists like me out for a generation. We're in danger of losing a huge piece of our cultural inheritance to thugs and looters, if we haven't lost it already. During the *illegal* American invasion of Iraq in 2003, the Iraqi National Museum was sacked by a rag-tag mob of bandits. Over 170,000 priceless artifacts disappeared, perhaps forever. Our military, by the way, didn't lift one finger to stop it."

Stuart clicked the remote gripped in his pudgy fingers and a statue of a winged bull with a human head appeared on a projection screen at the front of the hall. A tall crown and long, braided beard lent the ancient creature a regal bearing.

"The god-king, Nebuchadnezzar — gone missing after the invasion. Where do you suppose he is? In hiding? In paradise? Melted down for scrap? The copper alone is worth enough to feed an Iraqi family for months."

Stuart stopped next to the screen. "But all that's about to change. Three months ago, I asked the State Department for permission to go to Iraq. Yesterday, I received their reply." He paused, eyes twinkling. "Tomorrow I leave for Mesopotamia."

There was a smattering of applause.

"Once there, I will to do everything in my power to save your inheritance." He shook his head. "God knows the Army won't to do it. And it looks like the world's finest military needs all the help it can get!"

The class laughed again.

"I'm going to miss you, this campus, morning lattes at the University Center," Stuart smiled wistfully, "but when you joust with the devil, you're gonna get a little dusty. If reason doesn't battle corruption and superstition from time to time, it becomes just another meaningless catechism, and the world already has enough of those. Consequently, this will be my last lecture." He quickly added, "At least until next semester!"

The students burst into polite applause.

"I'll miss you all very much!"

The ovation followed Stuart to the exit.

He said over his shoulder before leaving, "Doctor Abramson will be here on Thursday to finish the semester. He's tough! If I were you, I'd stay two chapters ahead. One sacrificial lamb from this class is enough. Goodbye and good luck to all of you!"

*****

Minutes later, Stuart sat across the desk from his department chairman.

"Damn it, Frank!" He slapped the only open spot on the cluttered desk. "I'm going to Iraq! I'll be the only spade-and-brush man in the whole damn country doing field work in the war zone. That's gotta be worth something!"

The chairman shook his head. "Stuart, you're preaching to the choir. I admire your moxie, I really do, and I was happy to endorse your proposal. But it doesn't change a thing. Tenure is out of the question. This is your last semester. Dead issue. Case closed."

"Right. Not enough field experience. As if half the professors in this department ever got their fingernails dirty —"

"I said it was *one* reason. You haven't published in two years. Your TAs teach most of your classes. And since you brought up the other professors, yes – they say you're impossible to work with. You hardly attend committee meetings and when you do, you just piss everyone off. Trust me. I get the complaints!"

He paused, looking out the window. "And then there's the drinking…"

Stuart stared at the floor.

The chairman leaned forward, his voice a whisper, "What happened to you, Stu? You were so promising. So damn talented. We stole you from Stanford because we thought you'd set the world on fire. You just fizzled! Look, you're barely forty. It's not too late to save your career. Just start playing the game, okay? And damn it, play by the rules!"

"I'm sorry. I know I've disappointed you. But I also know I can do something special out there. And when I do, at least reopen my file. Frank, I can put this school on the map!"

Frank gave Stuart a hard stare. "Okay. I'll keep you on sabbatical while you're gone. We'll reevaluate your position when you get back. But, beyond that, I can't promise anything."

"Thanks, Frank. You won't be sorry."

"Make sure I'm not." They stood and shook hands – not as old friends, but like two boxers after a match.

"And Stu-"

Stuart paused in the doorway. Frank continued, "I served in 'Nam. I know something about…well, what's waiting for you out there. Nothing can prepare you for what you'll see. Nothing. Just be careful, Stu. Come back in one piece. Tenure isn't everything."

*****

Late that night, Stuart shuffled back and forth between drawers and bags in the warmly lit study of his spacious house in Sequoyah Hills, an upscale suburb of Knoxville. It was Stuart's crash pad after a nasty divorce and the loss of his prestigious teaching position at Stanford. As newlyweds, Stuart and his ex-wife traveled through the Smoky Mountains and were beguiled by the area's natural beauty and Old-Confederate southern charm. He fell in love with this place like the secret rebel he was – victim of that same bellicose mix of blind loyalty and rugged individuality that had cost him tenure, his wife, and the bright future in academia he viewed as a lifetime get-out-of-jail free card, or at least a hall pass excusing him from the harsher side of reality.

That grand horizon now seemed farther from him than ever. He wasn't sure, looking down at his army surplus duffel bag, if he had what it took to cross back over the River Styx to the land of the living…and tenured.

Mentally, he went through the few things he still had going for him. The U.S. government paid well for civilians who spoke Arabic, Kurdish or Farsi. They needed battlefield translators and cultural instructors and even the "non-tenured" could apply. Stuart's Arabic wasn't great, but he knew ancient Middle-East history better than most Muslims. He'd had offers to do field work in Cairo and the Sudan, mostly from second-tier non-profits, but could never bring himself to abandon the privileged life of academia to seek absolution in the desert. And purification — of biblical, koranic proportions — was exactly what he needed now. Professionally. Personally. Desperately.

He glanced again through a whisky-induced fog at the State Department pamphlet governing per diem, subsistence, and baggage. *One checked bag and one carry-on? For three whole months?* As for the checked bag, he'd already filled the duffel to bursting with shirts, jeans, underwear, toiletries, a thick book titled *The Archaeology of Ancient Mesopotamia*, and twenty pairs of socks. Frank, the chairman once told him that, next to his rifle, an infantryman's best friends were dry feet. Hidden among the socks were another rifleman's lifesaver: three half-pint bottles of Jack Daniels Black — purely for medicinal purposes. *No booze in Muslim countries.* He shook his head.

He tried to close the bag. No go. He tried again, mashing down with his knee as he worked the clasp, but his fingers gave out before it caught. He flopped into the wheeled leather chair behind his desk and loosened his belt. *Story of my life!*

An antique grandfather clock struck two. *Five hours until takeoff.* Stuart poured himself a drink from a half-empty bottle of Maker's Mark he'd saved for such an occasion. He downed the drink, grabbed the phone, and punched in the area code for Palo Alto, California. It took three tries to get it right.

"Hello?"

"Hey, Babe! It's me, Stu."

"Stuart? What do you want?"

"Just wanna talk. Are you busy?"

"It's eleven o'clock on a Tuesday. I'm in bed."

"Sorry. I wanted, you know, to tell you some things…Just in case."

"In case what?"

"I'm leaving for Iraq tomorrow."

"Did you join the Army?"

Stuart laughed. "Nah. I volunteered to be a translator."

"Why in the world did you do that? I thought you hated the war."

"Long story. Listen, can I talk to Rachel?"

"She's asleep…Jesus, Stuart! Have you been drinking?"

"How is she? How are you?"

"Like you suddenly give a damn after three years? Whatever's going on, it's not about Rachel. Or us. It's about you…As usual."

"I just want to tell her goodbye. It might be my only chance."

"You're not doing this, Stuart. You're not doing to her what you did to me. She's only five. Besides, you're drunk."

"Damn it, I'm not drunk!" He lowered his voice, "I just want –"

"You don't know what you want. You never did. You're a selfish asshole!" She sighed. After a long pause, she said, "I can't do this again. Be careful, Stu. I gotta go." Dial tone.

Stuart slammed down the phone and kicked his desk. He gritted his teeth and went back to the bag, trying again to shut it. Nothing. He punched the clasp until his knuckles bled. Some things, he guessed, you just can't force.

He collapsed into his chair and poured another drink.

2

Northeastern Iraq

Hadi was doing what he did best – exploring the moonlit hills east of his father's poor farm. Of course, these evening ventures were secret. What father permitted a ten-year-old son to climb alone in those dark, jagged rocks – a sacrificial lamb in search of an altar?

To Hadi, though, it was all high adventure. He especially loved finding new caves. Whenever he entered one, he *knew* he would find the lost treasure of his hero, the Kurdish warrior Salah ad-Din. Like other proud Kurds around the city of Tuz, Hadi knew the legend was no myth – just another forgotten truth.

The sun glinted in Hadi's hazel eyes as he knelt at the opening of his latest discovery. Cool air from the cleft flowed onto his face. He switched on his father's old flashlight and watched the beam disappear in the floating motes. The opening was narrow – just large enough for a slim boy to squeeze through. He put the light in first. Next went his head.

The small crack in the crusty ground opened into a chamber so vast it consumed the feeble light and left him breathless. His heart raced. Adrenaline ignited his spindly limbs like kerosene on a desert fire.

He squeezed through the entrance. His sandaled feet found gritty dirt. He crept through the void, following the flashlight's narrow spot until reaching a wall. It was cool and rough. He followed it to another corridor. This one branched off, going deeper. More cautiously now, Hadi edged onward.

The walls closed around him. The passage opened to another chamber, this one with walls smooth as his own goose-pimpled skin.

The heart of the mountain!

He scanned the room with the flashlight, feeling the presence of something ancient just outside the beam. Something old. Something sublime and unsettling. Something staring back at him.

Hadi dropped to his knees. The flashlight rolled against a polished wall. He touched his forehead to the floor between outstretched hands.

"Insha Allah. Insha Allah!" he whispered, chanting like his life depended on it. "God wills it! God wills it!"

*****

Camp Doha
Kuwait

Stuart wondered if the troop seat in the crowded, stinking cargo truck lumbering toward the airfield was made of steel or concrete. One thing was sure: the specs called for whichever was harder. He took a crumpled letter from a cargo pocket. It bore the gold-embossed letterhead of the U.S. State Department. Stuart read it for the hundredth time.

Congratulations, Dr. Knight. You have been awarded a 90 day contract as a civilian attaché to the Coalition Provisional Authority (CPA) in Baghdad, Iraq.

You are assigned TDY to the 2rd Battalion, 157th Brigade Combat Team, Tennessee Army National Guard, Forward Operating Base Bernstein, Iraq.

In addition to your duties as cultural attaché in the Office for Reconstruction and Humanitarian Assistance (ORHA), you will translate as directed for coalition forces in contact with indigenous personnel in the region.

Attached, please find forms and releases necessary for the processing of any death, dismemberment, or disability claims you, your family, or heirs may submit as a consequence of this service.

Stuart put the letter away. *Death, dismemberment, disability.* He was already wondering if his clever scheme to save his career by saving the ancient world was a mistake. The jury was still out – and would be for another ninety days.

His trek had begun with a commuter flight from Knoxville to Atlanta – the usual jumble of bored flight attendants and tired, shoeless businessmen. From there, it was another twenty-five hours to Kuwait City on a chartered jet packed with soldiers in desert cammo. They seemed calm for combatants returning to a war zone. They were more like college kids reluctantly returning from spring break.

On final approach, midnight local time, Stuart looked out the window to see the Kuwaiti capitol glowing in the desert night – an island of light in a sea of Stygian sand. Somewhere in the void beyond lay his final destination.

Illuminated spokes radiated from the shining metropolis as far as the eye could see. He thought they were highways, but as the plane descended, Stuart realized they were pipelines coursing with petroleum from Kuwait's oilfields – arteries carrying blood to the nation's throbbing heart. He stowed his laptop, stretched his ossified limbs, and prepared for landing.

The notorious Kuwaiti heat punched him in the face as he stepped from the plane. The hot ocean breeze reminded him of his boyhood in Southern Florida – except for the tangy smell of sulfur that thickened it to a paste.

Your petro-dollars at work, he sniffed.

Stuart followed the GIs into a hangar where a sergeant checked every name against the manifest. After a chorus of "Hooahs", the soldiers ambled outside to a bus convoy bound for Camp Doha, the logistical hub in Kuwait.

Stuart dragged his tired ass aboard a bus, feeling more like an imposter than a civilian, but was grateful to find padded seats, tinted windows, and air conditioning. The cabin lights were off. The curtains were drawn tight. A U.S. soldier armed with a rifle – locked and loaded – sat in the front seat, silently eyeing his comrades as they filed in.

Stuart took a window seat and peeked outside as the convoy lurched ahead. The thoroughfares they passed resembled those of any American city. Traffic, overpasses, reflective green highway signs, and the planted medians all looked reassuringly familiar. The only hint that they weren't in Kansas anymore was the Arabic writing above the English. He had always admired that graceful script, denoting, as it did, a culture that valued beauty as well as learning. Now it just looked alien and threatening, like gang tags on an L.A. street.

The convoy was escorted by American Humvees to the front and rear. Kuwaiti police cars filled the gaps throughout – blue lights flashing like a political motorcade. But it was the dust-colored "jeeps" with their angry gun turrets that brought the reality of this new world home. This wasn't TV. It wasn't a movie. This was a place where bullets and blood were real and the night belonged to the strongest.

His bowels grumbled. He looked for a restroom, but only bored or distracted vets – most of whom didn't look old enough to drink – looked back at him. Without a latrine, as the GIs called it, the long ride was about to get a lot longer.

I wouldn't be the first newbie to shit his pants in a war zone.

As the convoy left Kuwait City, smooth asphalt and bright lights gave way to rough roads and endless desert night. Through the slit in his curtain, Stuart watched the bouncing headlights of the busses behind him as the Saracen moon took command of the pitch-black sky.

Two hours later, the spotlights of Camp Doha blinded him and he closed the shade.

Departing the bus, Stuart passed a shoeless Arab kneeling on a piece of cardboard, his hands clasped in prayer.

Say one for me, buddy, Stuart thought. He didn't know if the shoeless wretch or the wretched academic would need Allah's help first, but he wouldn't mind going to the head of the line.

A beefy sergeant scanned Stuart's ID and directed him to the base orientation and transportation briefing. Instead of the all-night convoy to Baghdad he expected, Stuart learned he would fly to Iraq in two days. These days, flying was safer than driving, and even a small advantage like that was worth the wait.

The transient housing area was huge — at least the size of the Knoxville campus. It had thousands of twenty-man sleep tents, a phalanx of bathroom trailers, and a mess hall. That was it: a muggy dustbowl he would call home for the next two days.

A flatbed truck piled high with duffel bags arrived. A grizzled sergeant with a clipboard called out, "Baggage detail! Corporals and below, offload that gear!"

Half the soldiers in the group sprang into action. Within seconds, a hundred duffels pounded to the sandy ground. Stuart watched carefully for his bag, but it was a losing game. Unlike the other bags that bore stickers, coon tails, even a unit patch or two, his kit had no marks to distinguish it. Being a veteran apparently meant more than knowing the bad guys from the good. Even in the lesser arts of war, Stuart realized, stumbling among the dwindling pile of OD bags like the carcass of a half-devoured beast, he had a lot to learn. *And a flashlight would've been a good idea.*

As he flopped and twisted bags, he felt the sand — fine as powdered sugar — working its way into his nose, his lungs, his hair, into every fold of his clothes and crease of his body.

Finally, Stuart's was the last bag standing. He hoisted it onto a weary shoulder and set out to find a bed.

The sleep tents were filled on a first-come, first-serve basis. Being the last to find his duffel, he discovered all the nearest tents were full. It was after two in the morning – 0200, as the GIs put it – when he finally found a bunk. The tent was air conditioned, which was something, but the inside was still stuffy. He could only guess what it was like at noon.

This wasn't in the brochure.

After visiting the GI toilet, it was his stomach's turn to grumble. His last meal had been somewhere over the Black Sea and he knew the mess hall was open all night. He needed a drink too, but cocktail lounges in Kuwait were few and far between.

Stuart opened his duffle, pulled out his sleeping bag, and set aside some things for a shower after "dinner." He dug out the MP3 player he'd purchased for the trip, tried on the ear buds, and turned it on. He winced and turned down the volume.

Finally, something that works!

He removed the buds, put the player on his pillow, and turned to go.

"Better be securing dat."

Stuart jumped. He hadn't noticed the muscular Polynesian lying in the next bunk, still as a crocodile.

Stuart asked, "I beg your Pardon?"

The GI lowered the tatty paperback he had been reading and gestured at the MP3. "You putting dat away or it walking away."

"I'm just going to eat. I'll be right back."

"Okay. Suit self."

Stuart paused, "You mean somebody might steal it? I thought this was an Army post!"

"Be locking up anyting wit legs…And everyting got legs. First ting you learning in Army."

Stuart shoved the player in his bag. "I thought *al-Queda* were the bad guys."

The islander's tattoo-covered arms bulged as he rolled out of bed. Stuart looked up at him like a camper surprised by a bear.

"I…I'm sorry," Stuart said. "I didn't mean *you* could steal it. I've had a long day. No offense."

The soldier put a thick finger in Stuart's chest. "Only one thief in da Army. Everybody else just trying ta get their shit back. Savvy?"

Stuart stammered, "Sa...Savvy."

The big man laughed, revealing a shark-like gold incisor. "Don't sweat it." He reached for his cammo jacket hanging on the corner of his bunk. "I hungry, too. C'mon. I buying you dinner."

It was then Stuart saw the big man was a sergeant. The nametape over his breast pocket read "Babauta."

Stuart smiled nervously. "You're the man. Lead on."

After a meal of boiled vegetables and chicken seasoned too heavily with turmeric, Stuart skipped the shower and collapsed on his bunk. The sergeant had been friendly enough until Stuart shared his views on the war, then he got quiet as a shellfish. "Professor, you about ta get educated," were the sergeant's only words before going back to his book.

When Stuart awoke, Babauta was gone. He looked at his watch – 0815. The tent was already like an oven set to broil. Sweat ran down his face and neck, tickling his back. His sleeping bag was soaked. He sat upright and felt as if someone had shoved a rusty bayonet into his sinuses. The islander had warned him about it in the mess hall. He called it the "Kuwait Crud." Most people, even the lucky ones, got it their first time "in country." Unlucky ones got it the first day.

At least Stuart knew now on which side of the fence fate was going to put him.

After breakfast, Stuart rode a packed, stuffy camp shuttle to the clothing warehouse to sign for his equipment. He fell in at the end of a line at the long, dust-covered counter of a brightly lit supply room. The shelves behind were stocked with open-topped boxes of Kevlar body armor, helmets, canteens, and other sand-colored gear whose function he could only guess.

Stuart was studying the boxes when a snarky specialist snapped, "Let's go, buddy! We ain't got all day!" He waved Stuart forward.

"First time in theatre, old-timer?"

Stuart nodded. *Old-timer?*

In academic circles, Stuart was one of the youngest bucks on the block. Now, he suddenly realized he was the oldest man in the room.

"What size body armor?"

Stuart shrugged. "No idea."

The specialist glanced at Stuart's belly, bulging over his brand new L.L. Bean belt, and called over his shoulder, "Extra large! No — make it a double!"

Stuart blushed and sucked in his gut, but he still couldn't see his belt buckle.

The soldier slid a navy-blue armored vest across the counter. "Try this, Granddad."

Stuart picked it up. Its heft pulled him off balance. "What's this thing weigh?"

"Twenty-five pounds. Here's a hat to go with it." He tossed Stuart a blue helmet. Inside was a web of straps and clasps he was apparently expected to adjust himself. It was almost as heavy as the vest, and neither was equipped with air conditioning.

Next came a web belt, vinyl canteen, green canteen case, metal canteen cup, camel pack and padded suspenders that looked like Dirty Harry's shoulder holster, ammo pouches – despite the fact he was forbidden by the state department to carry a weapon – boots, more socks, an earplug case minus the earplugs, tinted goggles, and Nomex gloves, which he rather liked, but couldn't imagine wearing in this heat. They also gave him a plastic bag to hold it all – it split as he went out the door.

Back in his tent, Stuart dumped the gear onto his bunk and realized the only thing he hadn't been issued was an instruction manual on how to use it. Deciding where to start was like tackling a Rubic's Cube – an Army IQ test. After a few minutes of cursing and fumbling, a soldier a few bunks down took pity on him and helped Stuart piece things together.

Finally, he was ready for the fashion show. The kit was awkward and cumbersome. His steps were heavy. He felt like an astronaut walking down the gangplank toward his first launch. The vest's thick ceramic plates creaked like Dorothy's tin man in search of his oil. He felt like a toddler, banging into every bunk. Soldiers playing cards blinked up in disbelief and gave him a wide berth, like a leper.

Stuart plopped breathlessly onto his bunk. He gritted his teeth as tears welled in his eyes.

What the fuck have I gotten myself into!

Sure, all this junk might just save his life. He carried no weapon, but would face all the hazards of those who did. He may have been a peacenik contractor, but to anyone with an AK47 and a hard-on against America, he was now just a walking bull's eye.

And a slow one at that.

3

At 0600 the next day, Stuart rode in the back of a cargo truck to Doha's airfield and boarded an aging, cloud-gray C130 Hercules turboprop. He congratulated himself on elbowing to the front of the line until the plane's loadmaster directed a platoon of sweaty, armor-clad grunts to jam every seat on the bench, mashing him against the forward bulkhead to make room for cargo pallets. He was a sardine in a very small can, sautéed in sweat and gun oil. The cargo door clanked up and he felt claustrophobic as well as nauseous. He labored for breath, but his body armor mashed his chest. His helmet had already given him a splitting headache, and the chinstrap pinched his neck. If this was what going to war was like, Stuart wondered why history was so full of it.

A young marine, wedged so close that he was nearly in Stuart's lap, slumped low to make them more comfortable. "Tough shit on the seat, man." He smiled. "I wondered why you were in such a big-ass hurry to be first. Your first time in the sand box, right? Lemme tell you something: Don't go first, don't go last, and don't volunteer for shit. First thing you learn in boot camp. By the way, where are your ear plugs?"

Stuart flicked the plastic container dangling from his vest. "They just gave me an empty case."

The marine offered him a fresh soft-foam set, "Here! I got plenty. Always carry spares."

"Thanks." Stuart pinched the fluffy plugs into cones and shoved them into his ears. The muffled sound just made his claustrophobia worse. He gave the private a rictal grin and a half-hearted thumbs up and held a steady grimace during the two-hour flight.

Just as he nodded off, Stuart felt the deck fall away and grabbed the rigging over his head. He looked wide eyed at the load master, who was strapped into his own much more comfortable nylon seat on the bulkhead behind the cockpit.

"Combat approach!" The loadmaster yelled over the sudden decay of the engines, "We spiral down – corkscrew dive!" He made a spinning motion with his finger. "Makes us harder to hit from the ground!" He laughed. "Hope you had a big breakfast!"

The air pressure surged. The "crud" in Stuart's ears made his head feel like it would explode.

The big plane plopped on the runway. The great fans surged into reverse, throwing all of them against their seat belts. After a short taxi, the tail gate dropped, flooding the cabin with hot air.

Stuart disembarked and found his duffel – now marked with bright blue tape.

He hurried to the sleep tents and quickly found a comfortable bunk. He was learning the system. Now he just had to wait – no one could say how long – for the convoy to Forward Operating Base Bernstein, seventy miles due east.

Troops had more freedom at Camp Speicher than at Doha, so he caught the base shuttle and got off at the PX to kill time until lunch began at 1100.

Next to the PX, Stuart found a cluster of small shops – all in air conditioned container units – offering everything from a dry-cleaning to fast food burgers.

What's a war without a shopping mall?

He was attracted first by the local coffee house. The sign in front read "Green Bean's Coffee" – the Army's equivalent of Starbuck's. Blessedly indoors, it offered soft music and air conditioning. He ordered a latte and sat at one of the café's two small tables. He took a sip then remembered he was still wearing his borrowed ear plugs, so he removed them. *Latte*, he mused, quite pleased with the way a bad morning was turning out, *lends dignity to what would otherwise be a vulgar brawl.*

The mess hall was a mile away, but he was happy to stretch his legs. He passed the phone center near the shops and briefly thought about calling California, but walked on. He arrived safely and was alive and well. It was better to imagine somebody caring about it than proving once again that she did not.

The mess hall was a circus tent, its canvas big top suspended by wires and poles, with hardwood floors and drywall inside. The size of a football field, it looked like it could hold a battalion. Televisions lined the walls. Flags from of every state and U.S. possession hung in tidy rows from the rafters like a medieval banquet hall. Even in an alien desert, it was hard to not feel at home.

Stuart crab-stepped through the chow line like a veteran, grabbing a plate of roast pork and broccoli. It was the best food he'd eaten since Club Novela, and there wasn't even a bill. For dessert, he dug into a mound of Baskin-Robbins ice cream.

If casualties were on the rise here, it sure wasn't due to starvation.

A young soldier sat next to him, squared a tray of hot food and asked, "Borrow the pepper?"

"Be my guest!" Stuart passed him the shaker and asked, "Where do you come from sol-"

The blast blinded Stuart and threw him from his chair.

His eyes opened onto a gash in the canvas roof. Twenty state flags fluttered down like confetti. Tables and benches were overturned. Chairs lay strewn everywhere. A hole in the floor smoldered ten feet away. The stench of burned powder and charred flesh filled his nose. Everybody seemed to be running in his own silent movie.

Almost everyone.

The soldier that had been beside him was on the ground, grabbing the knee above a calf that lay half-way across the hall. Blood gushed from the ragged stump. He was screaming, but all Stuart heard was the ringing in his ears.

He stood shakily and braced himself on the table, now covered in syrupy blood. His vest and hands were splattered with gore. He looked over at his wounded tablemate. The trooper's head now lolled at a grotesque angle, his cobalt eyes dead blue. It was then that Stuart noticed that his neck was missing down to the spine. No more blood pumped from the wound – his strong, young heart lay still.

Stuart felt someone touch his arm. A female medic peered into his face. Slender thumbs lifted his eyelids. She was shouting like somebody hailing a cab.

"What?"

"Are you wounded?" The medic's voice was now faint, but audible.

Stuart just stared at her, glassy-eyed.

She yelled, "You're okay! You got lucky! Mortar round misfired! Stay put!" She hurried over to the next casualty.

But Stuart couldn't stay put. He stumbled outside on shaky legs. Looking down, he discovered he'd wet himself. He took a few more steps, then fell on all fours and vomited.

Soldiers continued to run in and out of the shattered mess, ignoring him.

Still trembling, Stuart ran to his tent. Stifling at midday and without air conditioning, the place was empty. He went to his bunk, tore off the sweaty, bloodstained vest and shirt, stuffing the shirt in the trash. He then rifled frantically through his duffel until he found his treasure – one of the three half-pints he'd packed for the trip.

He downed the first with hardly a pause for breath. He trashed the bottle and reached for the second, uncapped it, then his knees gave out and he sat heavily on the bunk. Like a watchmaker, he carefully screwed the cap back on, secured it safely near the bottom of the duffel, then rolled unconscious onto his bunk.

*****

The next morning, Stuart awoke to dust-covered cargo trucks and up-armored Humvees braking next to the sleep tents. Stuart's head throbbed as he donned a clean shirt and heaved his duffle bag onto one of the trucks. His pants, vest, and boots were still flecked with blood, but nobody seemed to notice – or care.

"Doctor Knight?" A tall lieutenant held out a hand.

Stuart nodded and shook it.

"You're riding with me in the lead Humvee. We roll in five."

Up front again. The hairs rose on Stuart's neck. He considered asking about yesterday's mortar attack, about the casualties, about the tactical situation, but nobody seemed concerned.

As he walked to the Lieutenant's Humvee, Stuart realized he was getting the VIP treatment. The other convoy passengers – mostly soldiers returning from leave – were clambering into the open-topped cargo trucks. Their sides were protected with shop-made armor plate, but any Arab kid with a grenade and a decent pitching arm could turn their human cargo into spaghetti. *Why the hell doesn't anybody mention the mess hall?* Stuart climbed into the back seat, still in a daze. Gears grinding, they were off.

The convoy straddled the centerline as it navigated out of Camp Speicher to city streets lined with cheap shops, palm trees, and trash. All other traffic – cars, donkey carts, kids on bikes, and old folks with canes – were forced to yield.

Seeing Stuart's blank expression, the lieutenant explained the rules. "When a hajji gets too close, the nearest gunner waves him off. If that don't work, he aims at the driver and shouts. That usually does the trick."

"What if it doesn't?"

"He puts a few rounds through the engine block." He winked, "That *always* gets their attention."

Stuart sank into his seat. For years, he'd told his students that American tactics were heavy handed. He railed against this kind of "jackboot justice" since the war began – it only recruited new insurgents. Now, he wasn't so sure. The line between necessity and hypocrisy, between here today and gone tomorrow, seemed precariously slim. In these crowded, shoddy, sweltering streets, even in the safety of an armed American camp, it seemed virtually invisible.

Beyond Tikrit, the scrubby farmland became open desert, dotted here and there with palms and mud-brick huts.

The sun beat down on the convoy, turning open-topped trucks into roasting pits and Humvees into Dutch ovens. Stuart fumbled with the passenger door and asked the lieutenant, "How do I put my window down?"

"You don't. That's four-inch-thick bullet-proof glass. Won't give you much protection if it's open."

Stuart tried to relax. He hadn't eaten in almost a day and remembered some snacks he had bought at the Speicher PX. He reached for the plastic bag holding a chocolate bar and bottled water. The chocolate was tar. He tossed it on the floor by his boots and pulled out the water. The plastic bottle was cab-temperature. The first gulp went down like motor oil. It must have shown on his face.

The lieutenant took a big swig from his canteen, belched, and wiped his mouth with his sleeve. "Gotta stay hydrated." He grinned. "Give it another try. You'll get used to it. Nothin' like the taste of hot plastic in the mornin'!"

They crossed the Taoq Chay River on a pock-marked concrete bridge and continued to the foothills of the Qandil Mountains. After another hour, the convoy took a sudden left off the rough hardball highway.

Stuart asked, "What's wrong?"

The lieutenant pointed down the road. "IED! It's sittin' on our turn! We gotta cut through this field!"

The Humvee crossed the rocky patch, then headed north on a washboard trail for two more miles.

"There ya go!" The lieutenant punched Stuart's arm playfully and pointed ahead. "We made it!"

Dead ahead lay the wire-ringed berm of F.O.B. Bernstein.

*****

Binoculars dropped from narrow eyes as the convoy disappeared behind the Bernstein gate. They rose again and shifted back to the ordnance disposal team at work in the intersection.

Excellent. Everything is going as planned.

Like any skilled hunter, he was used to studying his prey. Learning procedures. Searching out patterns. Spotting weakness.

The Americans' weakness was his strength. They would feel it soon. It would be sudden, without warning, like a bolt from the blue. A bolt of holy lightening.

4

As the convoy approached Bernstein, Stuart could tell this base was smaller than Speicher or Doha. He took in its entire width in a glance. Guard towers sprouted from its earthen berm perimeter at regular intervals. Concertina wire spread in concentric rings around the base for several hundred yards. In the distance, black smoke plumes rose from the oil fields of Kirkuk. The scene had a post-apocalyptic feel.

After security halts at the outer and inner gates, the Humvee came to rest. The long journey was over.

Stuart sighed with relief as he pulled his aching body from the cramped vehicle. His foot caught the doorframe and he hit the ground face first. He got to his knees, trying to wipe fine sand from his sweaty face. He looked like a sugar cookie.

"Humvees can be a bitch."

A shadow fell across Stuart. He looked up to see a huge figure standing over him.

"Doc!" It was Babauta. The imposing islander pulled Stuart up and dusted him off. "Why you not telling me you come here!"

"It never came up."

The sergeant laughed and slapped Stuart on the back. "Hungry?"

"Starving."

"Good! Hope you liking chicken."

He put Stuart's duffel in a Humvee and drove them a short distance to a cinderblock building coated with earth-colored stucco in the middle of the base.

Babauta guided Stuart through a curtained doorway, "Da hajji shop! Best chow north of Baghdad."

The shop was furnished with multicolored plastic tables and chairs. European techno music blared from a television in the corner. The succulent smell of chicken and lamb roasting over the open flames of the restaurant's brick oven permeated the space. Everything from cheap brass souvenir lamps to digital cameras and MP3 players were displayed on rough wooden tables and secondhand racks. Two tables in the back were dedicated to bootlegged DVDs and CDs. It reminded Stuart of a border town cantina.

Stuart asked, "Hajji shop?"

"Yeah. Run by locals…hajjis."

Stuart winced at the politically incorrect term.

Babauta showed him to a table occupied by two soldiers. He pointed to them and said, "Da battalion intel team."

The first soldier barely looked eighteen. He was rail thin with olive skin and an infectious smile.

"Dat's Specialist Vasquez. Junior man. 'Being in less dan a year."

Stuart smiled politely, "Good to meet you."

Next was a grizzled sergeant with a serious expression. "Dat's Sergeant Parson. Twenty-year vet. Senior intelligence sergeant."

Parson shook Stuart's hand.

"Welcome to Bernstein."

"Thanks. Good to be here."

Parson held his grip. "Hands soft as butter. Must be a college boy."

Stuart pulled free, smiled and pointed to his head. "I work with this."

"So why are you here? Ain't any civilians bein' drafted. You volunteer?"

"I did."

Parson's eyes narrowed, "Why'd you go and do a thing like that?"

"Just wanted to do my duty."

Parson looked skeptical. "You met Captain Allen yet?"

"No. Who's that?"

"Battalion intelligence officer."

"What's he like?"

Vasquez answered, "Don't mess with Captain Allen. He don't take no shit."

Parson pointed at the young trooper. "Watch yer mouth."

"Sorry Sarge." Vasquez turned back to Stuart. "You'll know Allen when you see him. He's the only dude on base with one leg."

Stuart was surprised. "One leg?"

Parson answered, "Allen was here with his active duty unit last year – One Hundred First Airborne Division. His Humvee was hit by an IED.

The door blew open and threw him clear. The rest of the crew burned up. Allen was the only survivor. Lost his leg below the knee."

"How is he still on duty?"

"He spent the rest of his tour rehabin' in Germany. He swore he wouldn't go home till he caught the bastard that killed his men and took his leg. Worked his tail off to get cleared for duty again. When he did, his unit was already back in the States, so he found out which unit was serving in Tuz and volunteered."

An Iraqi man arrived with plates of roasted chicken, fried potato slices and naan bread. "Here you are, my friends!"

Babauta introduced the waiter, "This Ayad. He own da shop. We calling him Ed. He Taking good care of us. Good guy."

"Thank you my friend. You are too kind." Ayad asked Stuart, "Would you like chai?"

"Sure. I'm always up for trying something new."

The food smelled delicious. Parson bowed his head. The other soldiers followed suit as Parson said grace. Stuart bowed his head too, although he wasn't sure why.

I haven't done this since I was nine.

Stuart tasted the chicken. "Wow! This is great!"

Babauta smiled. "Told ya."

Parson said, "I hear you're a subject matter expert. What's your background?"

"I teach archaeology at the University of Tennessee."

"What good is that? We're fighting a war, not digging up bones. You speak Arabic?"

"I do."

"That's helpful. It'll be good to have an American around to make sure our local translators are shootin' straight with us."

"Is that a problem?"

"Sometimes."

"How do the locals feel about Americans?"

"Most of 'em like us. I'd say ten percent support us by serving in the Iraqi police, army, and the like. Just a few work against us."

Vasquez handed Stuart a soda can adorned with Arabic writing.

"Thanks." Stuart opened the can. "What about the rest?"

"They ride the fence. They wanna back the winnin' team. They're worried we won't stay to finish the job – just tryin' to survive. I'd probably do the same."

Stuart was dying to ask, "So how do you guys feel about the war?"

Parson replied, "You ever read the Old Testament, Doc?"

"A little."

"Brother's been killin' brother here since the beginning. Always will. The place is cursed."

"Then how can we achieve victory?"

"Victory," Parson said somberly. "Victory is makin' sure my son don't come back to fight the next war." The veteran sighed, "All I can do is my duty."

"Duty? Don't you ever feel like you're being used…manipulated?"

"I don't always agree. It's my duty to voice my objections. But after that, I still have to follow orders, like 'em or not…as long as they're moral and legal."

Stuart shook his head. "I don't get it."

"Guys like you never do…At least not until you learn to love something more than yourself."

Stuart bristled then said with a smile, "Spoken like a true crotchety old bastard."

Parson laughed. "I like you, Doc. I don't know why, but I do." He clapped Stuart on the shoulder. "It's time you got settled in and cleaned up. You gotta be tired after your trip. And besides, you stink."

Stuart laughed. "True."

Parson called to the islander, "Sergeant Babauta, take Doctor Knight to his quarters." Stuart stood. Parson grabbed his arm and said, "You got guts, Doc, but be careful. I don't know what you're here for, but it ain't worth dyin' over. Your little girl needs her daddy."

*****

Brad Baxter stood in the battalion command bunker. He was deep in thought as he studied a large map that covered an entire wall. "2nd battalion, 157th Brigade Combat Team, Tennessee National Guard Area of Operations" was written in block lettering across its top.

Baxter studied dots on the map that marked the locations of every IED encountered by the battalion. He was trying to find a pattern – trying to get inside his opponent's head.

Baxter was the leader of Bernstein's explosive ordnance disposal team. His call sign was Boomer.

The last IED was a decoy. He had examined the components before sending it to the explosives lab in Tikrit. It would be weeks before he heard back from them, but he already had what he needed.

Baxter checked his watch. Colonel Thorne, the battalion commander, was supposed to meet him here fifteen minutes ago. This was his first time working with a National Guard unit. The atmosphere was too casual for his liking.

A private called to him from the radio desk. "Boomer, the colonel's having lunch at the hajji shop. He wants you to meet him there instead."

Baxter shook his head. "No. We have to talk in private."

"He insists, Sergeant."

"No. The hajji shop's got ears all over the place."

The trooper shrugged. "He said this is his Burger King, Sergeant. He gets it his way."

Baxter rolled his eyes. "Fuckin' National Guard."

5

"Here ya go, Doc." Babauta parked the Humvee by a cluster of containerized housing units near the berm. Each white aluminum box was surrounded on all sides by green sandbags stacked chest high. The entire quad was surrounded by fifteen foot tall concrete pylons.

Body armor, ammunition, soda cans, plastic lawn chairs, and coolers littered the ground. The dwellings were decorated with animal skulls and other grizzly trophies. Stuart couldn't decide whether the place looked more like a junk yard or voodoo temple.

"We calling dis P-quad." He pointed to an earthen berm nearby. "Close to da perimeter."

Babauta opened one of the units. The air inside the aluminum box wafted hot and stale in their faces. Stuart entered the small space and tossed his body armor onto the steel-framed bunk. The only other furniture was a metal chair and small desk. The room's two windows had rollaway shades, drawn to block the sun.

Babauta turned on a wall-mounted air conditioning unit. It wouldn't make any ground against the heat until night. "You getting VIP treatment. Dis usually having four guys." Babauta sat in the chair. "You sure making impressions!" He tossed the door key to Stuart.

Stuart heaved his duffle bag into a corner and sat on the bunk. The metal wires poked him through the thin mattress pad.

He sighed, realizing how tired he was. "I hope I didn't piss anybody off at the haj…at the shop."

"Na. You honest. Dey respecting you, even if dey disagreeing with you. But still… Better watching you mouth."

"How did Sergeant Parson know I have a daughter?"

Babauta shrugged. "He doing dat all da time. Da men call him 'Spooky' behind back, but I tink he knowing dat too."

"It is a little unsettling."

The sergeant checked his watch. "You washing up and settling in. I coming back at 1700. Walking you to T.O.C. for intel in-brief wit S-2."

"You'll be here when for what?"

Babauta chuckled. "Sorry, Doc. I speaking Army. I coming back at five 'n walking you to command center for brief wit Cap'n Allen, our intelligence officer."

"Okay. Thanks."

The islander smiled. "I liking you, Doc. You making me laugh." He walked out into the hot desert sun, closing the door behind him.

*****

Baxter found Thorne enjoying chicken shish kabobs and fried potatoes in the hajji shop. The colonel waved Baxter over.

"Have a seat, Boomer. What's on your mind?"

Ayad brought naan bread as Thorne wiped grease from his mustached lip.

Baxter answered, "We got a problem, sir. Al-Khayal has got his hands on some advanced stuff. He's changing the game. I sent the components from the last few IEDs to division for analysis."

"Khayal again. You should stop listening to Captain Allen. He's paranoid. What did division say?"

"They're backlogged. It'll be weeks before I get anything back."

Thorne smiled. "Then why get so worked up? Let's wait until we hear from division. No use getting everybody upset over nothing. Remember. We're here to keep the peace."

Baxter persisted, "He's sizing us up, sir. We gotta get him before he strikes for real. Shouldn't we at least tell the company commanders? They need to know if we have a new threat."

Thorne's smile dimmed. He didn't like being questioned. "We'll cross that bridge when we get to it. Get the facts first."

Captain Crumm, commander of Alpha Company, entered and sat next to Thorne.

Crumm looked at Baxter and smirked, "Who shit in his Cheerios?"

Thorne chuckled, "He's seeing ghosts again."

Baxter pressed his case, "Sir! Your men are in dange-"

"You're dismissed, Boomer. The captain and I have business to discuss." He turned to Crumm.

Baxter didn't budge. "Sir, we can't just-"

Thorne growled, "I said you're dismissed, *Sergeant*."

*****

Ismael carefully assembled the device. He always did. He didn't trust the others to do the job. They weren't believers. They killed for pay. He'd seen the type all too often. Most were from outside Iraq. Syrians, Egyptians, Saudis – mercenaries more interested in money, booze, women, and a soft bed than the will of Allah.

It wasn't about money for Ismael. The Americans had taken much from him. They had to pay. He fingered a scar that ran from his forehead across a ruined eye to his jaw. It happened twelve years ago, during the last war, but it still felt like yesterday.

Ismael was ten – huddled with his mother and five-year-old sister in the bedroom of the family's Baghdad apartment. Shouts from the streets outside mingled with deep thuds in the distance.

His father burst in the room. "Get up! The Americans are bombing the city! We must leave now!"

His mother darted around the house, grabbing her most treasured belongings. Her arms were full of keepsakes as his father hurried her to the door.

She turned back and screeched, "My mother's tea set! I must save it!"

The windows flashed. His father knocked the woman's bundle to the ground, "There is no time, woman! Go!"

Ismael was the first out the door, followed by his mother. They watched from the street as his father grabbed Ismael's crying sister and carried her in his arms. When they reached the doorway, the world disintegrated in dust, crashes and screams.

Ismael awoke moments later. He sat up and looked around. The city was dark. His home was gone. His mother lay unconscious – her arm half severed above the elbow. He looked for his father and sister, but couldn't see them. His ears rang. His left eye didn't work. He felt his face and withdrew a blood covered hand.

His mother moaned softly. Ismael scramble to her. "*Um!*" He cradled her head, thankful she was alive.

He scanned the ruins of his home and spotted a small hand protruding from the rubble. He gently laid his mother's head down and crawled to his sister. He clawed at the debris until he uncovered the girl's face. She was gone. His father's body lay next to her. He grasped the girl's hand. It was still warm.

Ismael cried out in agony. His head spun. His face seared with pain. He collapsed next to his sister. The flashes and thuds of the American bombs faded away as he lost consciousness.

His childhood ended that night. He became the head of his house. That was also the night he decided to join the Jihad. He would avenge his family. He would be a tool of Allah's holy justice.

Ismael wondered how different his life might have been had his father and sister lived, if he'd grown up tending sheep. Would he have had a family of his own? It didn't matter. Allah willed a different path for him.

Insha Allah.

He checked his watch. No time for reminiscing. There was much to do.

*****

Stuart stretched out on his bunk. It felt good to bathe and put on clean clothes.

After Babauta left, he ventured out in search of a toilet and shower.

He found the shower easy enough but it wasn't what he expected. The word 'shower' was an overstatement. It was a collection of home-made plywood stalls with water run to them from an open-topped cistern atop a nearby bunker.

He longed for the comparative luxury of Camp Speicher.

I'll bet there's no Baskin-Robbins in the mess hall, either.

Stuart stepped into a stall and closed the rickety door, locking it by rotating a board nailed to the frame. His nostrils were assaulted by a stench rising from the pool of stagnant water beneath the pallet floor.

Stuart hung his clothes over the wall. They were stained salty white with perspiration. He examined the showerhead and two round metal knobs, guessed which was for hot and gave it a few turns. The spigot sputtered, hissed and then spat a stream of warm, brown water.

Stuart considered putting his clothes back on, but this was the only shower. He didn't have a choice.

I may as well get used to it. I already stink anyway.

As he bathed, Stuart wondered if what he was washing with wasn't dirtier than what he was washing off.

After showering, Stuart spotted two green a port-a-johns.

Good idea.

He opened the door to one of the toilets. Once again, he was bombarded by foul odors. Stuart gagged and checked the other outhouse. Just as bad. The air inside had to be at least 120 degrees. Countless flies buzzed around him incessantly as he did his business, flying relays back and forth, between him and the filth below.

After the unpleasantness of the portable latrine, Stuart returned to his quarters to rest his aching limbs. The air conditioner still fought its losing battle against the heat.

His muscles relaxed and he began to drift off to sleep. There was a knock at the door. Stuart didn't budge.

Too exhausted to move, he called out, "Who is it?"

Babauta yelled, "Time for in-brief!"

It was a quick Humvee ride to the command bunker containing the intelligence office.

A tall, dour looking captain with a prosthetic leg met them at the door.

Babauta said, "Cap'n Allen, dis Doctor Stuart Knight."

"I'll take it from here, Sergeant." Allen dismissed Babauta and led Stuart to his office.

The walls were covered with maps, mug shots, and satellite photos. Allen closed the door and motioned Stuart into a white plastic lawn chair before limping to his own. "What do you think of Iraq?"

"Nice place. I might buy a summer home here."

Allen scoffed, "Why the hell are you here? And don't give me that duty bullshit you gave my guys."

Stuart forced a smile. "This is a great opportunity for an archaeologist."

"You teach at U.T., right? That's my alma mater. I still have friends there." He locked eyes with Stuart, "Good friends."

Stuart shifted uneasily.

Allen's gaze remained on the professor. "I made some calls. Let's just say your reputation ain't the best. I also know you pulled a lot of strings to get here. Then there's Stanford. Want to tell me about that?"

"Not really."

"Sounds to me like the only opportunity here is for you to save your ass."

Stuart said nothing.

"Doesn't matter. I don't give a shit why you're here as long as you do your job. But if you endanger any of my men, I'll shoot you myself. Got it?"

Stuart nodded.

"Good. I'll give all the info I can, but the best way to learn is on the ground. What do you already know about the Sunnis and Shiites?"

"I know they don't get along. The rift was created when Muhammad died in 632 A.D. without a son. Two men claimed to be Muhammad's successor. The Shiites backed one and the Sunni's backed the other. The feud continues to this day."

Allen nodded. "Good. What about the Kurds?"

"They and the Arabs hate each other."

"Do you know why?"

"Not really."

"It's all about Kurdistan."

"I've never heard of Kurdistan."

"It doesn't exist. The Kurds are a people without a country. They want a sovereign state and will do anything to get it. After World War I, the British redrew the map of the Middle-East without regard to ethnic or cultural boundaries." Allen pointed to a map pinned to the wall. "As a result, 50 million Kurds occupy an area containing parts of Iraq, Syria, Iran and Turkey. Tuz sits on the southern edge, right on the border between Kurdistan and Arab country. This whole area used to be Kurdish before Saddam Hussein drove them off and 'Arabized' it. Now they want their land back and the Arabs won't give it up. The Kurds are itching to reclaim their property and are willing to slaughter anybody in their way. They just need an excuse. Tuz is where it all comes together – a ninety thousand person powder keg one spark away from a bloodbath."

"Sounds to me like the Kurds are the good guys."

"Don't let sympathy for them cloud your judgment. Plenty wouldn't think twice about killing us if it helped them get what they want."

Stuart asked, "What about terrorists? We had to detour around a bomb on the way here."

Allen nodded, "That IED turned out to be a dud, but insurgent activity is on the rise. The targets have mostly been Iraqi security forces and civilians. Intel indicates the leader is an evil son of a bitch. No one knows his real name or even what he looks like. Iraqis call him *Al-Khayal*."

"Al-Khayal…The Ghost?"

"Yup. The locals think he's the fuckin' boogeyman, but he's just a gutless butcher."

"Is there anything else I should now?"

"Yeah. The most important thing." Allen pointed to the American flag on his shoulder. "Don't trust anybody unless they're wearin' one of these." He stood. "Class starts tomorrow. We're goin' to Tuz in the morning."

"I was hoping for some time to get settled."

"Like I said, the best way to learn is on the ground. The sooner, the better." Allen opened the door. "You're dismissed."

*****

Stuart's mind reeled as he left the command bunker. *Tomorrow?* This was all happening too fast. *Shit, it's hot.* He was suddenly aware of the day's furnace-like heat. "What now?" he said, wondering how to spend the rest of the day. P-Quad lay a few hundred yards across a scrubby field. Ayad's shop was about the same distance to his right.

Sweat ran down his back as he considered his options. He thought about taking a walk to explore the rest of the base, but quickly decided it was too damned hot for that. From what he'd seen, it was probably a fool's errand anyway. All the quad had to offer was sweat and boredom. Stuart's stomach was too nervous to eat, but a cool soda sounded nice. *The hajji shop it is.*

Stuart arrived at the shop and found it closed for the day. *Just my luck.* He sighed and started back toward the quad.

A Humvee pulled up next to Stuart as he walked. A soldier asked from the driver's seat. "Need a lift?"

Stuart smiled. "Sure! Thanks!" As he climbed aboard, he hoped this was a sign that his luck was changing.

"Where ya headed?" the soldier asked.

"P-Quad I guess. I was going to the hajji shop for a soda, but it's closed."

The trooper offered, "I'm goin' to the mess hall. You're welcome to join me."

"Thanks. Sounds good."

"I haven't seen you around here before."

Stuart replied, "Just got here today." He held out a hand. "Stuart Knight. Friends call me Stu."

The soldier shook his hand. "Brad Baxter. Friends call me Boomer." He glanced at his passenger's clothes. "You a contractor?"

Stuart nodded. "Yeah. Translator. I'm here for ninety days."

They parked next to a large plywood shack tucked into an old aircraft hangar. Stuart looked quizzically at Boomer. "This is the mess hall?"

Boomer explained, "Bernstein used to be an Iraqi air base. Hussein built it to guard the mountain passes east of here." He motioned to the hangar. "These things are made of reinforced concrete. Comes in handy during rocket and mortar attacks."

"Yeah." Stuart wished there had been a hangar at the mess hall on Speicher.

They entered to a familiar scene – a space bustling with soldiers eating, talking, and waiting in line for hot chow. But it wasn't all the same. GIs dished the grub here. This rickety facility didn't boast TV's or a salad bar. There was only one choice for a main course and it looked like shoe leather smothered in gravy. The sides were lettuce and boiled potatoes. There was no Baskin-Robbins.

Boomer waved Stuart to a table. The soldier picked at his chow and asked, "Where ya from?"

Stuart answered, "All over."

"Got a family?"

Stuart studied his food. "I used to. We're divorced." He shifted the subject from himself. "How 'bout you?"

"Yup." He pulled a picture from his pocket. "That's my wife, Sharon and our boy, Tommy."

Stuart noticed the pair in the photo both had yellow ribbons pinned to their shirts. He smiled and returned it. "Good lookin' family."

"Thanks. I'm going home to see 'em in a few weeks. I promised Tommy I wouldn't miss his birthday. I haven't seen him in six months." Boomer's eyes reddened. He took a deep breath and forced a smile.

"I haven't seen my daughter in a while either."

"What's going on back in the States?"

"Nothing much. Just business as usual."

Boomer shook his head. "That's what I thought. I watch the news from home. You wouldn't even know there was a war on. The only thing they ever mention is the body count. Politicians thump their chests and make speeches, but nobody really gives a shit about what we're doin'. Sometimes it makes me wonder why the hell we're here. She doesn't say it, but I know Sharon feels the same way. She sees it everywhere she goes. Makes her feel like she's all alone." He paused. "But you don't wanna hear me bitch 'n moan. Sorry man."

Stuart grinned. "No problem."

Boomer looked at Stuart's plate and asked, "Not eating?"

Stuart eyed the shoe leather with contempt. "I'm not hungry."

Boomer laughed. "Me neither. Let's go." As they dumped their trays, he said, "I'm going to the phone center to call home. Wanna join me?"

Stuart thought a moment and answered, "No thanks. Maybe next time."

The sergeant replied, "You sure? You're in the sandbox now. Might not be a next time."

The words gave Stuart a chill. "No. I'm good."

"Okay. Lemme at least give you a ride home."

"Sounds good."

When Boomer pulled into the quad, he said, "Stu, I've been on a lot of deployments to a lot of places, but this one's different. Something about this place gets inside you. It changes you."

Stuart eyed Boomer uneasily. "Thanks."

Boomer grinned. "I'm just saying this place changes everybody, but how we change is up to us. You have to make it for the better or it'll eat you up."

"Gotcha. Thanks again. Good to meet you, Boomer."

"You too." Boomer pulled off toward the phone center.

*****

"Hi, Sweetheart. It's good to hear your voice." Boomer sat in FOB Bernstein's phone bunker, talking to his wife. The small cement room was filled with echoing voices. It held the only eight phones on the base and had the acoustics of a racquetball court, but none of that mattered to him. It all faded away as soon as he heard Sharon's voice.

As his wife updated him on all the news from home, Baxter closed his eyes and let her comforting voice wash over him. It subdued his fear and calmed his frustration. Iraq melted away. He was home – if only for a little while.

6

Hadi sat on a stone with his shepherd's stick. He watched his father's sheep graze in the scrubby fields as the morning sun peeked over the mountains. The cave and what he's found in it consumed the boy's thoughts and haunted his dreams.

He reached into a cloth sack slung over his shoulder. He pushed his goat cheese lunch aside and pulled out a black stone figure. He held it with trembling hands as he stared into its face. The thing scared him. Its lion-like head was oversized and grotesque. Horns sprouted from a swirling mane. Fangs protruded from its gaping maw. But it was the bulging eyes that frightened Hadi most. They were cold and cruel, like a shark's.

What were the markings on its base? What did they mean? Hadi wanted to ask someone but he didn't know who.

He couldn't ask his father. Hadi would have to tell him where he found it. That would lead to confessing to being in the caves and stealing his father's flashlight. Besides, his father was just a poor farmer. He wouldn't be able to tell Hadi any more than he already knew.

He missed his mother in times like this – not that he ever knew her. She was more of an idea to him than a person. She died giving birth to him. His father never forgave him for that.

Hadi had an idea. "Faisal! I'll ask Faisal! He will know!"

Faisal was a local Arab merchant that Hadi knew well. The man was about Hadi's father's age – early forties. But, to Hadi, Faisal seemed wiser and worldlier than the old farmer. Faisal was well traveled. He knew about business, politics, and history and spoke several languages.

Yes! Faisal would surely be able to tell him exactly what he had found.

Hadi didn't care that his father forbade him from visiting Faisal. Like most Kurds, his father hated Arabs.

He thought again of his father. *Stupid old fool.*

*****

Sharon Baxter and her son, Tommy, were having lunch in a small restaurant half a world away. Each wore a small yellow ribbon over their heart with Boomer's picture at its center.

Sharon smiled at Tommy. "Excited about Daddy coming home?"

"Mommy, I'm worried about him. It's such a long way home."

Sharon reached across the table and held her son's hand. "He'll be fine. Don't worry. Just think of happy things. Think of how wonderful it'll be when we're all home together at your birthday party." She forced a smile. She had to be strong for her son.

She hoped Tommy didn't see through her. There was something in her husband's voice that worried her. He wasn't confident. He seemed shaken, even afraid.

Sharon looked at the other families in the restaurant. All smiling...All together. *You don't have any idea how lucky you are. You can see each other anytime you want.* They didn't have to worry about being maimed or killed. She faced that fear every day. *Don't you people know there's a war on? Doesn't anybody care?*

The waiter approached her table. "Your bill's been taken care of."

Sharon looked confused. "But who...?"

"The person wished to remain anonymous but wanted me to thank you for everything that you and your husband are doing for our country."

Sharon was stunned. Someone did care.

"Thank you so much." Sharon barely got the words out. She unconsciously touched the ribbon on her chest.

*****

Stuart climbed into the back seat of Allen's Humvee. "Let's tour Tuz! I can't wait to-"

"Change of mission," the captain interrupted. "There's an IED in the middle of town. It's on a busy street next to the biggest mosque in Tuz. Boomer's team is already on the ground. We're their backup."

Babauta climbed into the Humvee.

Stuart felt relieved. "It's good to see a friendly face."

Babauta smiled. "Somebody need covering your ass, Doc."

Allen raised the radio's hand-mic. "Let's roll."

*****

The predator surveyed his prey. The plan was working perfectly. As predicted, the American bomb disposal team had arrived and was preparing to deploy the robot. He knew them better than they knew themselves.

*****

When Allen's team arrived, the Iraqi forces had established an outer perimeter around the IED – desperately trying to hold back the curious crowd and mounting vehicular traffic.

American soldiers formed a smaller circle around the bomb. To Stuart, it seemed like every person in Tuz was there. The civilians, pressing closer for a better view, seemed totally oblivious to the danger. It was impossible to keep them out. Several penetrated all the way to the Americans' inner circle. More arrived each moment.

Allen said, "If this crowd panics, the shit'll hit the fan."

*****

A voice on a cell phone commanded in Arabic, "Begin phase two."

A white four door sedan emerged from an alley near the Iraqi perimeter. The fenders were painted bright orange like an Iraqi taxi cab. Distributed between the back seat and trunk were six 155 millimeter artillery rounds. Each one weighed fifty pounds and had a potential kill radius of three hundred meters.

The hunter watched the car from his perch. Ismael had recruited the driver from the slums of Baghdad. He couldn't recall the young man's name. It didn't matter.

The driver wore an explosive vest with a dead man's switch. If his thumb released the button in his right hand, the vest would explode. He seemed willing enough, but was handcuffed to the steering wheel in case of second thoughts. As usual, the artillery shells were also rigged to ignite if the door opened. As always, this detail was left out of the driver's pre-mission brief.

The taxi moved slowly toward the Iraqi perimeter. Neither the Americans nor their Iraqi allies noticed it at first.

Allen was watching the bomb disposal team attempt to disable the IED using a robot equipped with a water charge when a nearby Humvee gunner yelled, "Captain Allen! You need to see this!"

He shouted to the gunner. "What is it?"

The soldier pointed to the car. "There's a taxi forcing its way through the crowd, sir."

"If it breaches the Iraqi line, give him a warning."

"Yes sir!"

Babauta grabbed Stuart and said, "Stay close."

*****

Another phone call. "Prepare phase three. On my command."

The taxi was now among the Iraqi policemen. They aimed their AK74s at the driver and ordered him to halt. He didn't respond. His eyes never left his target. He began to chant, softly at first, then louder and faster.

"Allah-u-akbar, Allaah-u-akbar, Allaaah-u-akbar, Allaaaah-u-akbar!"

Then the policemen spotted the taxi's cargo and scattered. The Iraqi perimeter fell apart. There was nothing between the car and the Americans.

The gunner shot a five round burst at the ground in front of the car.

The driver screamed his chant at the top of his lungs. "ALLLAAAHHH-U-AKBAR!"

One more word from the cell phone unleashed hell. "Now!"

The IED exploded. The bomb disposal robot disintegrated instantly. Curiosity turned to terror. Confusion turned to chaos. The crowd turned into a stampeding mob.

Something caught Allen's eye. Not everyone was panicking. A man spoke calmly on a cell phone on a second floor balcony. His handsome face was marred by a nasty scar running across a milky white left eye.

Allen growled, "Al-Khayal."

The car sped toward the Americans. The driver knew his time was short. In moments, he expected to be in Paradise.

Babauta shoved Stuart to the ground. "Get down!"

Allen tore his gaze from the balcony and fired his pistol at the taxi. "Kill that son of a bitch!"

A torrent of lead slammed into the car as the American line opened fire.

Chunks flew from the taxi. Sparks sprang from the asphalt.

"ALLLLAAAAHHH-U-AAAAKBAA…!"

The driver's chant was cut short by bullet ripping through his neck. Blood peppered the interior of the car. His hand instinctively jerked it to his wound, releasing the dead man's switch.

The vest exploded. Windows shattered, spraying the street with razor sharp shards of glass. The soldiers shielded their eyes with their arms.

The car came to a halt. All was still. The soldiers lowered their guard to see what remained of the vehicle.

As Allen stepped forward, a shock wave hit him like a freight train. The artillery shells had detonated, sending the taxi twenty feet in the air in a gigantic fireball.

Babauta covered Stuart with his massive frame.

Allen tumbled through the air. His leg flew off midflight before he slammed to the ground.

Babauta yelled, "Medic!"

Stuart looked up to see Allen still on the ground. The captain wasn't moving.

7

Allen opened his eyes. Something was different. He sat up and looked around. Everything was gone. The crowd, his men, the mosque, the city. All gone – replaced by a featureless, barren landscape.

He got to his feet, then realized he had two of them. He stared down in disbelief. He was whole.

Allen heard crackling behind him. He turned and saw a Humvee engulfed in flames. He moved closer, but felt no heat. His gut knotted as he reached out to touch the burning vehicle – unsure if it was real.

"It's all your fault," a ghostly voice whispered.

Allen looked around, but saw no one. "Who's there?"

"You let us die," the voice said.

Allen shouted angrily, "Who are you?"

"You know who we are," the spectral speaker said once more.

Allen looked to his right. There were three of them – faces blurred in shadows. They wore American uniforms. The eagle of the Hundred and First Airborne Division glared from their shoulder patches – its beak stretched open in a muted shriek. The captain stepped closer. Recognition hit him like a five-ton truck. "Buck? Is that you?"

The center specter nodded.

"But…You're dead."

*****

"This is really something, Hadi! Where did you get it?"

Faisal and Hadi sat in the Arab's shop in the market district of Tuz. The streets were deserted. Everyone had gone to see the bomb.

Faisal's shop was tucked away in a side alley, blocked from all but a few rays of sunlight. It was dark, stuffy, and hot. Brightly colored rugs hung along the walls. Sculptures and other trinkets – replicas of ancient treasures – were displayed on racks in the storefront.

Faisal handled the statuette gently. If authentic, it could be valuable – extremely valuable.

"I found it in a cave near home. I knew there was something special in those hills!"

"Can you show me?"

"Sure! We can go there now!"

Hadi swelled with pride. Faisal took him seriously. Hadi felt important. He felt like a man. He got into Faisal's car and triumphantly led the way. This was the best day of his life.

The cave's entrance was too narrow for Faisal due to the extra forty pounds around his midsection. He had to widen the hole by digging, kicking, and scrapping before gaining passage. It was still a tight squeeze.

By the time they got to the chamber, Faisal's pants and silk shirt were torn and dusty. Bloody scrapes showed on his elbows and knees.

"Allah be praised." Faisal's voice was barely a whisper. He couldn't believe his eyes. If he played his cards right, this find would make him a wealthy man – but only if this discovery remained a secret. If word got out, it would spread like a fever. The hills would crawl with treasure hunters. No, he had to ensure his fortune remained hidden.

"Are you sure you haven't told anyone else about it?"

Hadi shook his head. "I haven't breathed a word."

The beam of Faisal's flashlight turned on Hadi. His voice was ominous. "Unfortunately for you, it must stay that way."

*****

Allen recognized the second shade standing before him. He barely looked eighteen. His nametape read "Stubb."

The young apparition said, "I never got to see my baby girl."

Another voice whispered, "We tried to tell you, but you wouldn't listen."

The third figure, named Flask, raised a horribly burned hand and pointed at Allen.

The whisper echoed again. "You didn't believe us. We told you Al-Khayal was real. Do you remember what you did?"

Allen put his face in his hands. "I...I laughed."

"You laughed. We died."

Buck grabbed Allen and pulled the captain's face to his. "You killed us!" His flesh melted and began to fall from his face. His eyes burned in their sockets. "YOU KILLED US!" The phantom burst into flame.

Allen felt the flames lick his flesh. "I'm sorry!" The fire engulfed him. He tried to step back, but fell. His leg was gone again – below the knee was a bloody, ragged stump.

The three hellish shadows descended on him, grasping at his limbs.

Allen's flesh bubbled under their touch. He watched his own flesh fall from his bones. He screamed, "I'm sorry! I'm sorry! I'll kill him! I'll make him pay!"

The dead men thrashed him mercilessly as the whisper turned into a shriek. "You killed us! YOU KILLED US!"

"I'm sorry!" Allen woke with a gasp – his face a picture of terror.

A medic knelt over the captain shaking him gently. He asked, "You okay, sir?"

Allen regained his senses, "Yeah…I'm okay."

"You don't *look* okay."

"I'm fine, dammit. Anybody hurt?"

"None of our guys but you, sir. Some civilians are messed up. The hajji in the car is gone to Allah."

Allen tried to sit up. "We gotta reestablish our perimeter and get support down here. Where's my leg?"

The medic put his hand on Allen's chest. "Just a minute, sir. You have a concussion."

Allen brushed him aside, grabbed his prosthesis, and strapped it in place.

He stood and scanned the balcony where the one-eyed man had been. Empty.

He called for reinforcements and medical support, and then hitched around the perimeter, personally checking each trooper.

Stuart watched the crowd scatter – dissipating like vapor. He saw the twisted piece of scrap that was the taxi. Pieces of it and its victims littered the ground. The injured, dead, and dying lay everywhere.

Allen pointed to the scene and called to the medic, "We got wounded! Let's go!"

Stuart ran to Allen. "I'm going, too!"

"Suit yourself."

At the scene of the blast, Stuart witnessed a panorama of slaughter. The ground was covered with charred bodies and scraps of rent flesh.

They worked quickly – helping those they could. Many were women and children.

Boomer went along to check for unexploded ordnance.

A man ran up to Stuart carrying his son in his arms. The child was limp. He laid the child at Stuart's feet. The boy looked about eight years old.

The man cried uncontrollably, "You fix my boy! You American! You can fix!"

Stuart knelt over the boy and saw that the left side of his head was missing.

"You fix! You are American! YOU FIX!"

Stuart fell back onto his haunches, his face white. He didn't know what to do.

"I, I'm sorry. I can't fix. I'm sorry."

The man exploded in rage and grief. He grabbed Stuart's body armor vest with both hands and screamed, "NO! YOU CAN FIX! YOU AMERICAN! FIX MY BOY!"

Stuart stared blankly, apologizing in a barely audible voice.

Boomer broke the two apart and leaned over the boy. "How bad is he?"

Stuart didn't answer.

Boomer saw the wound. "Oh, God."

Babauta grabbed the pair by the collar. "We going now!"

Boomer nodded. "Yeah. Okay. Let's go."

Boomer's team took pictures of the scene and collected what pieces of the bomb they could find before heading back to base.

The sun was low in the sky as the patrol returned to Bernstein. Allen dismounted without a word and hobbled to the command bunker.

Stuart stepped from the Humvee and wretched. He wiped his mouth and asked Babauta, "How do you do it?"

The sergeant leaned against the Humvee. "Just do. Thinking later."

*****

Ismael sat silently in a darkened room of his safe house staring out the small window on the opposite wall. The smoke from his cigarette hung about him like a burnouse.

Sulayman Bak was the perfect hiding place. The Arab town wasn't friendly to Americans and was big enough to blend in easily.

The attack in Tuz was a failure. Not one American died. Worse yet, Iraqis were killed. Ismael was comforted in knowing they were in Paradise – the most recent unsuspecting martyrs in his jihad.

He cursed the driver, "Ignorant fool."

The idiot panicked, sure enough, but it wasn't completely his fault. Ismael thought of the American captain that spotted him on the balcony. There was hatred in the soldier's stare. He wasn't like the others. He was unpredictable. He adapted and broke the pattern. He was a hunter. That was a problem.

Ismael had to adapt, too.

The next attack must be simpler. More focused. More specific.

He had an idea. "Yes." He dialed his cell phone.

*****

Boomer found an isolated spot behind his bunker and stole a rare moment of privacy. He struggled to keep his composure as the day's events replayed in his mind. He watched the sun through moistened eyes as it dipped below the horizon.

He reached into his pocket and pulled out a picture of Tommy that he always carried with him. He hadn't seen the boy in almost a year. He wondered if he would ever see him again. He felt helpless and small.

Boomer fell to his knees, holding the picture tightly against his chest. He wanted to see his son, to hold him and know that he was safe. He couldn't hold back any longer. Sorrow overcame him like a flood bursting through a dike. He stayed there, alone in the sunset, crying tears of heartbreak only a parent can know.

8

Stuart's stomach was in knots as he lay in his bunk that night. He was drenched with sweat, but it wasn't from the heat although his room felt like a toaster oven.

The explosions. The screams. The smell of smoke and blood. The dead eyes.

Could he get used to it? Did he *want* to?

He'd been in Iraq less than a week, but had already seen more death than most do in a lifetime.

He dug the second flask of Jack Daniels from his duffel and guzzled it down. He hoped it would help him sleep. It didn't.

He tossed and turned as his mind churned. Morbid memories mingled with fears of the future to paint pictures of doom and despair.

What if he was next? He'd never given much thought to his own mortality. After years of studying the religious beliefs of other cultures, Stuart found it ironic that he had none of his own.

Did he believe in God? His mind said no, but his heart wasn't so sure.

His stomach lurched again.

Did the soldiers feel like this? What would he feel two months from now?

Stuart hoped he would live to find out.

*****

The next morning, Faisal raced toward the mountains north of Tuz. He was livid. Not only had the little brat escaped him in the cave, but he also stole the statuette from his car. Faisal tried in vain to relocate the cave's mouth since dawn. After hours of sweating in the merciless sun, his frustration boiled into rage. The boy had hidden the entrance. His head throbbed from a knotted gash on his brow – courtesy of a rock jutting from the cave wall. The outcropping had knocked him out cold as he pursued Hadi the day before. He would have caught the boy if not for it. The boy would pay.

He was on his way to see Hadi's father. The time for games was over. Either Hadi would guide him back to the cave, or Faisal would kill the boy and his entire family.

He smirked. *Even if he does, I'll kill them all anyway.*

*****

Stuart and Captain Allen travelled the road to Tuz. The engine droned as the sun beat down from a cloudless sky. The stifling air in the Humvee smelled of sweat, metal, and oil.

Stuart noticed a series of holes along the roadside. As he approached each cavity, he craned his neck, looking for a bomb. His pulse slowed as each passed only to rise again with the approach of the next seconds later.

Then Stuart saw it in a hole to his right – an artillery round.

It flashed. In the fraction it took for the hell fire to reach him, a thousand thoughts sped through Stuart's mind. He thought of his life, his home, and his family. Most of all, he thought about his wife and daughter.

I'm so sorry.

He was blinded as the searing light enveloped him.

"No!" Stuart sat bolt upright in his bunk. He was covered in sweat.

Just a nightmare.

Thump! Thump! It was the noise that woke him. Someone was banging on his door.

He checked his watch. It was almost noon.

"Doc! You okay?" Babauta was yelling through the door.

Stuart answered, "Yes! I'm fine! Come in!"

The islander entered. "How you sleep?"

Stuart rubbed his eyes. "Not well."

"Nobody sleep good here. Not shit right either. Dis place mess with your gut."

Stuart stretched his back. "Yeah. I noticed. What can I do for you?"

"I takin' you to lunch. Guys already dere."

"Lunch?"

"Hurry. Get dressed."

Stuart pulled on some jeans. "Are you sure they want to eat with me?"

Babauta smiled. "C'mon, Doc. We going."

*****

Hadi sat on a hill overlooking his family's small mud brick home. He enjoyed watching his father's sheep. It was a good place to think. The object of his thoughts rested in his small hands. The statue was both wonderful and horrible.

"What are you? What is your secret?" He knew the object held the key to some ancient truth. He also knew it was dangerous.

Hadi was glad the cave was narrow and dark as he thought about his narrow escaped. He didn't even have time to grab his father's flashlight. Hadi just ran as fast as he could into the familiar hills until his lungs felt like they were on fire. He was lucky to be alive. He was just as lucky his father hadn't found out.

He knew he was dead if Faisal got his hands on the treasure. Hadi had to give the merchant a reason not to kill him. Hiding the cave's entrance was all he could think to do. Hadi hoped it was enough to keep him alive. Faisal would have to keep his golden goose alive if he wanted more treasures. But even then, how much time could that really buy him?

He looked down onto the fields and saw his father at the plow behind the family's donkey, tilling the soil. His countless warnings about Faisal echoed in Hadi's ears, growing louder with each reverberation.

"I will never defy you again, Baba."

Faisal often belittled Hadi's father for his lack of sophistication. He called the man an ignorant farmer, barely able to scratch a living from the dirt.

Hadi used to agree with him. Now he was ashamed. He saw the man differently. The ignorant laborer was now an honest, wise, hardworking father who only wanted the best for his son. Hadi wanted to be just like him.

He hoped he would feel the same after his father discovered the flashlight was missing. He put the statue into a cloth sack with his lunch and slung it over his shoulder. Then he spotted a dust plume approaching in the distance.

As the vehicle drew near, he recognized Faisal's silver BMW. Hadi knew this moment would come, but he still didn't know what to do.

Dust flew as Faisal's car ground to a halt next to Hadi's father. The merchant sprang from the vehicle and slammed the door.

Hadi's father stopped plowing and walked cautiously toward the angry visitor. He knew this man. He had a bad reputation. Smuggler. Thief. Stinking Arab.

"What do you want?"

Faisal demanded, "Where is Hadi?"

"Why do you want to know?"

"He has stolen something from me. I have come to get it back."

"What did he steal?"

"That is not your concern."

"He is my son. That makes it my concern. What proof do you have?"

Hadi had worked his way down the hillside – careful to stay out of sight. Faisal's back was to him.

Faisal grabbed something from the passenger seat of his car.

"Your little thief is stealing from you as well as me." Faisal threw the flashlight to the ground at the farmer's feet. "Does this look familiar?"

Hadi saw his father's expression change from indignation to rage and disappointment.

Faisal hissed, "Yes. I think we understand one another. Where is the boy?"

"I will deal with this. Tell me what he has stolen from you. I will see it is returned."

Faisal knew Hadi still hadn't told his father about the artifact. "I told you. This is between the boy and me."

"I have tolerated your disrespect long enough. Get off of my land."

"Not without the boy!"

The men stood toe to toe.

"I said leave! Leave now and never come back, you stinking Arab criminal!"

Faisal struck Hadi's father in the face, knocking him to the ground. Hadi started to run to his side but his father's eyes shot him an unmistakable message of warning.

No, Hadi! Get back! Hide!

Faisal pulled a pistol from the small of his back and aimed it at the farmer's face.

*****

Stuart and Babauta joined Parson and Vasquez in the hajji shop at their usual table.

"I'm sorry about the other day." Stuart held out his hand.

Parson took it and smiled. "Don't sweat it, Doc. You're right. I *am* a crotchety old bastard. Let's eat."

Several Iraqi soldiers entered followed by a tall, broad built man wearing a black beret and a thick, Saddam Hussein style mustache.

Parson whispered to Stuart, "That's Colonel Saffa, the commander of the local Iraqi army battalion."

The Iraqi swaggered to the back of the souvenir shop and waited there, staring at Ayad.

Ayad approached Stuart's table. He carried plates of food in shaking hands. "Hello, my friends."

Parson asked, "What's wrong, Ed?"

"Nothing. Nothing my friends." He forced a smile. "I must go. Enjoy your food." He walked slowly to Saffa.

Vasquez asked, "What the hell's that about?"

"Not sure. But it don't look good." He glanced at Vasquez. "And I told you to watch your mouth."

"Sorry Sarge."

The Americans watched Ayad take the cigar box containing the day's revenues from under a table and hand it to Saffa. Ayad handed over a wad of money from his shirt pocket as well.

Parson's eyes narrowed. "What the hell is he doin'?"

Saffa put the money into two stacks, one twice the size of the other. Ayad stood meekly as Saffa pocketed the larger stack.

Saffa smiled broadly. Ayad bowed submissively and thanked the Iraqi commander. Saffa strolled smugly out the door.

Vasquez stood and stepped toward Saffa.

"No." Parson grabbed the young soldier's arm. "Saffa may be Iraqi, but he's still an officer. It's gotta be handled by another officer. I'll let the colonel know about this."

Babauta spoke quietly as the last of Saffa's entourage trailed out the door, "I hearing he Republican Guard before war."

Parson nodded. "He was an intelligence officer. I fought the Republican Guard in '91. Saw what they did to the Kuwaitis. You know what 'intelligence' meant in the Republican Guard? Rape, torture, and murder."

Parson went on. "I'll tell you another thing, too," He pointed to his forehead. "You know that crest on his beret? That's the symbol of the Republican Guard. He wears it right in front of us. The son of a bitch is rubbin' our noses in it."

Stuart asked, "Have you told the colonel?"

"Yeah. I told Colonel Thorne. He said I was 'mistaken.' He said it was the symbol of the new Iraqi Army. But I'm tellin' ya. I was here the first time. I fought the bastards. I saw what they did. I'll never forget that crest."

*****

Boomer and Allen stood in Captain Crumm's quarters. Boomer implored Captain Crumm to intervene and convince the battalion commander that Al-Khayal was a real threat to his men.

Boomer said, "You gotta talk to Colonel Thorne for us. It's no secret you're his favorite. He'll listen to you."

Crumm sat silently in a lawn chair as Allen paced the room – his artificial leg squeaking with each step.

"Yeah. I'm the golden boy," Crumm said as he leaned back in his seat. "The old man listens because I don't feed him shit like you're giving me right now."

Boomer showed Crumm a stack of photos. "These are components from yesterday's IED. Advanced stuff. Same stuff I tried to tell the colonel about. Damn near impossible to disarm."

Allen stopped pacing and tossed Crumm an intel report. "The stuff's coming in from Iran through the mountains east of town. That's in your sector."

"How do you know it's coming through *my* sector? It could come from anywhere along the border."

Allen pointed to the report. "Kirkuk, Tikrit, Baquba – All have seen devices like this. Tuz sits in the middle of them like the hub of a wheel. The mountain passes east of Tuz – the ones this airbase was built to guard – are the only crossing point for a hundred miles. It all adds up."

"Coincidence."

"If you believe in coincidence, you don't belong in intelligence."

Crumm tapped a finger on his desk. "Okay, I'll talk to Colonel Thorne."

"Thanks," Boomer said.

Allen eyed Crumm suspiciously then left without a word.

Crumm pulled a cell phone from his pocket after both men were gone and dialed. "We have a problem."

9

Hadi's father was still on the ground. Faisal's eyes glared as he stood over him, pointing the pistol at the powerless man. Faisal roared, "One last time! WHERE IS THE BOY?"

Faisal put his foot on his victim's chest to demonstrate his dominance – to tell the Hadi's father he was lower than the dust under his feet.

Faisal's aunt ran from the hut and shielded the farmer with her own body.

"He doesn't know! Neither of us knows! We haven't seen him for days!"

Faisal laughed. "You use your woman as a shield. Disgusting." He spat on them. "I'll be back. Next time she won't be able to save you."

Faisal moved closer and stood over the couple. "And so you know I mean what I say…" He stomped the farmer's hand. Bones snapped. Hadi's father gritted his teeth, but didn't cry out.

Faisal sped off, peppering the couple with dirt.

Once Faisal was gone, Hadi ran to his father.

"Baba! I'm sorry!"

The backhand hit the boy so hard that he spun in the air before hitting the ground.

"WHAT HAVE YOU DONE? YOU HAVE KILLED US ALL!" His father was screaming so wildly that he was barely understandable.

Hadi sobbed, "I'm sorry. I'm so sorry."

"You brought this on us. We are disgraced. Get out. GET OUT!"

Hadi ran as fast as his legs could carry him. Tears soaked his face. He didn't know where he was going. He had nowhere *to* go. He had no family, no friends, and no home.

*****

Boomer trudged into Ayad's shop and plopped down at the table with Stuart and the others. He said with a sigh, "Fuck this place."

59

Parson asked, "Did you and Captain Allen get Crumm to talk to the old man?"

Boomer cut his eyes at the veteran. "How did you kno-?" He shrugged. "I don't know. He said he'd help, but it didn't sound very convincing."

Stuart asked, "Why wouldn't he help, especially after the car bomb?"

Boomer said, "Cuz Crumm and Allen hate each other."

"Why?"

"Allen is active duty like me. He plays by the book. Shortly after getting to this unit, he conducted an inspection and found out Crumm had lost a bunch of equipment and didn't report it. It was some serious stuff too – rifles, pistols, night vision goggles, heavy machine guns. Rumor was the stuff made its way to the black market. It should have ended Crumm's career."

"Why didn't it?"

"Thorne covered the whole thing up. I'm sure you've heard how close Crumm and the colonel are. It ended up almost costing Allen his career."

"Sounds like Captain Allen's had a tough time lately."

"Yeah. Shame too. He's a damn fine officer. I served with him on active duty before he lost his leg. He was a different person then."

"How so?"

"We were in Korea. He was a lieutenant. I was a buck sergeant. He was one of the nicest guys you'd ever meet. The troops loved him. He was fair, quick with a joke, and damn good at his job. He's still a damn good officer, but different." Boomer sighed again. "This damn place changes everybody."

*****

Faisal sat in the shade of his shop that evening, smoking a cigarette. The market district around him was closing down for the evening.

He had experience selling items on the black market. He could make a fortune in Hadi's cave.

But I must possess the treasure before I can sell it.

Faisal smiled. He had Hadi where he wanted him. If Hadi didn't give Faisal what he wanted, Faisal would kill his family and torture the boy until he told him what he needed to know. Then the brat would die.

60

On the other hand, if Hadi did as he was told…

They will still die.

As usual, Faisal would get what he wanted. The result would be the same either way.

*****

Stuart returned to P-quad to find a soldier with mouth full of chewing tobacco sitting in the chair next to his bunk thumbing through his copy of *The Archaeology of Ancient Mesopotamia.*

He asked, "Who are you?"

"Captain Lester Crumm." The intruder held out a hand. "Just came by to introduce myself."

The teacher cautiously took the hand. "Stuart Knight. How did you get in here?"

"I go anywhere I please on this base."

Stuart forced a smile. "What can I do for you, Captain?"

"I heard you met Allen and his gang." Crumm tossed the book onto the bunk and spat a glob of tobacco juice on the floor. "What'd you think of 'em?"

Stuart shrugged. "They're soldiers."

Crumm smirked. "Very diplomatic. You're a smart guy, Doctor Knight. A guy like you knows how important friends can be, especially in a dangerous place like this. Choose yours wisely."

Stuart answered plainly, "Thanks. I will."

Crumm stood and spat again, splattering Stuart's shoe. "I'll be seein' you, Doc. Count on it." He strolled out the door, leaving it wide open.

Stuart wiped up the spittle and shut the door. He couldn't help but to feel once again that coming here was a very bad mistake.

*****

Captain Allen sat in his office vigorously composing a sketch of the face he'd seen on the balcony in Tuz when Boomer appeared in the doorway.

The explosives expert said simply, "I'm out."

Allen looked up and furled his brow. "What are you talking about?"

"I've done a lot of thinking since the car bomb."

61

"And?"

"I'm through looking for trouble. It finds us well enough on its own."

"So you're quitting on me."

"Our little talk with Crumm today was useless. He ain't gonna help us. Nobody is and you know it."

"Nobody said it would be easy."

"Look, man. I got three weeks left before goin' home. Al-Khayal ain't my problem anymore."

"Is that what you're going to tell the family of the next guy Al-Khayal kills?"

"I'm not playing a game I can't win. Don't you see? We can't do it alone." Boomer looked at Allen's drawing. "Like I said, I'm leaving next month. Why don't you leave too? Go back to Fort Campbell. See your family. Leave this shithole behind."

Allen was unmoved.

"Don't give me that look." Boomer rolled up his sleeve to reveal a nasty, puckered burn scar covering most of his arm. "Remember this? I gave my pound of flesh too. We're both lucky to be alive. Be thankful! Quit while you're ahead and go home!"

"I can't do that."

"You're a fanatic."

"Maybe it takes one to catch one."

"Fine. Suit yourself. Chase your demons all over Iraq if you want, but I won't be a part of it anymore. I'm doin' my job for the next three weeks and that's it! You can hunt Al-Khayal alone."

"Understood," Allen replied curtly.

Boomer started out but paused at the door. "You've changed. When that IED went off, that bastard took more than your leg. Every day you chase him, you give him a little more. Killing him won't get it back. If you give him enough, he wins…This place wins. I'm tellin' ya as a friend. Quit while you can. There are no happy endings here."

Allen simply stared at Boomer.

"You didn't hear a damn thing I said." The sergeant shook his head. "Good luck."

Boomer left Allen sitting in silence.

The captain pulled a photo of his wife and son from his pocket and studied it fondly. With loving tenderness, he gently traced their faces with his finger. He sighed and put the picture in its place.

Allen sat staring into space for a long moment. He looked reluctantly over his shoulder into the corner of the room. Three charred figures stood there in silence. Under the weight of their unflinching gaze, Allen returned to his sketch.

*****

Hadi sat alone on a hill overlooking Tuz. He didn't know what to do. He was in a mess and couldn't see a way out. He pulled the figurine from his bag and raised it over his head, ready to smash it against the rocky ground.

Blinking back tears, Hadi reconsidered. The statute was all he had to bargain with. Destroying it wouldn't solve anything.

The afternoon call to prayer echoed over the arid landscape. Hadi knelt obediently, the idol clenched tightly in his little hand.

When he arose, his choice was clear. He nodded to the arcane figure. "Yes. It is the only way." He would offer the statue to Faisal. Perhaps he could convince the man to spare him for the promise of more treasure. Maybe the Arab would be merciful. Maybe it would be enough to save his life – or at least the lives of his family.

He would worry about it in the morning. His fate could wait until then. Tonight, he was just a boy alone under the stars.

It was in God's hands. Hadi could, at least, find some peace in that. *Insha Allah.*

10

Babauta and Stuart sat in the hajji shop early the next afternoon. Half-eaten plates of chicken and fried potatoes sat in front of them.

"You ready, Doc?" Babauta stood and slung his rifle.

"Yeah. I guess." Stuart grabbed his helmet and bulky body armor.

"You liking Tuz. Lots of history and shit."

"We're meeting the police chief right?"

"Yup. Colonel Hagir."

"What's he like?"

"Making Cap'n Allen look like girl scout."

Stuart rolled his eyes. "Wonderful."

Babauta laughed and punched Stuart's arm playfully, knocking him off balance.

"Doctor Knight! You are going to Tuz?" Ayad appeared with chai for them.

Stuart nodded.

The Iraqi smiled. "Good luck, Doctor. Colonel Hagir is a good man. You will like him."

"I'm sure I will." Stuart downed his chai and handed Ayad some Yankee dollars. "Here ya go. My compliments to the chef."

Ayad declined, "No, my friend. It is my pleasure." He grabbed some colas from a stand-up cooler and handed them to Stuart and Babauta. "Here. For the trip. Be careful, my friends."

The two thanked Ayad and walked to the command bunker to meet Captain Allen.

They arrived at a scene buzzing with activity. Soldiers were testing radios, checking rifle magazines, and tending to other pre-mission tasks as the wind swirled sand around them. The patrol's three Humvees were already loaded and ready.

Vasquez stowed his M4 carbine in Allen's Humvee and waved to Stuart before climbing into the driver's seat.

Stuart watched the rest of the men as they finished their last checks and mounted their vehicles.

Stuart suddenly felt vulnerable. He didn't have so much as a letter opener on him. He pulled Allen aside. "Can I have a gun?"

"If it gets to the point that *you* need a weapon, were already fucked."

Stuart spotted a large, black handled knife attached to Babauta's body armor. "May I borrow your knife?"

Babauta shook his head. "No can do. Father giving to me. He carrying it two tours in 'Nam. It protecting me."

"Superstitious?"

"When everyting outta control, you taking any help you can get."

Stuart caught a glimpse of Vasquez kissing a rosary before slipping it back under his shirt.

No atheists in foxholes.

Stuart pondered the difference between faith and superstition. Was there a difference? Was faith just superstition in prettier wrappings? The academic in him said it was, but a distant, muted part of Stuart told him it wasn't that simple.

Sergeant Parson ran up to Stuart. "Just wanted see you off on your first trip to town. I gotta stay here and mind the store."

"Thanks. Wish me luck."

"Ain't no such thing as luck, Doc. We're all in God's hands." He patted Stuart on the shoulder. "Don't worry. You'll be fine."

"I hope you're right."

Parson smiled. "I am. See ya when you get back."

The sergeant trotted to Vasquez. Stuart couldn't hear what he said, but saw them bow their heads to pray.

Stuart said to Babauta, "Those two are pretty close."

"Yeah. Parson promising his momma he taking care of him 'n getting him back safe. Getting under da kid's skin sometimes. He calling Parson mother hen."

Allen pulled a pair of goggles from the carrier that hung from his hip. Keeping the lens covered, he turned them on briefly to test them.

Stuart asked, "Are those night vision goggles?"

Allen nodded as he checked his ammo pouches. "Yup."

"It's the middle of the afternoon."

Allen was annoyed. Stuart had interrupted his pre-mission ritual. "We're *hoping* to be back before nightfall, but there's no guarantee. Now shut your hole and mount up."

Stuart took the seat behind Allen's. Babauta got in the opposite side.

The islander handed Stuart a set of earplugs. "Putting dese in."

Stuart declined, "No thanks. These Humvees aren't *that* loud."

Babauta grabbed Stuart's wrist and pressed the spongy stoppers into his hand. "Not for Humvee. If IED hitting us, noise shredding da eardrums."

Before leaving the base, every weapon in the convoy was test fired between the inner and outer gates. A guard approached, beckoning to Stuart.

"Sir, you need to exit the vehicle and test fire your weapon."

"I'm an unarmed civilian contractor." In spite of believing himself above such adolescent bravado, Stuart was embarrassed to admit he wasn't packing.

The trooper shrugged. "Suit yourself, buddy. It's your funeral."

As the convoy left Bernstein's outer gate, Stuart's hands began to tremble.

The cramped, stuffy confines of the Humvee smelled of diesel fuel, dust, and sweat. The odor and constant jostling conspired with the heat to make him feel as if he would be sick at any moment.

Stuart scanned the landscape as they trundled along. Both sides of the road were dotted with circular holes. Stuart warily eyed each one as it passed, trying to ignore his mounting sense of déjà vu.

Vasquez pointed to a pile of stones stacked precariously on top of one another. "Those rock piles are all over the place here. Don't know what the hell they're supposed to be. I chalk 'em up to board sheep herders."

Stuart saw the stones too. "They're markers. They can represent anything from property boundaries to irrigation patterns. The method has been passed down for thousands of years. Ancient Egyptian farmers used a similar method to mark property boundaries along the Nile. They utilized the technique in creating the study of geometry."

Vasquez yelled over his shoulder, "No shit?"

"No shit. The word 'geometry' is Greek for 'to measure the earth.'"

Stuart smiled. It felt good to play teacher again. He was afraid he wasn't making a very good pupil.

Stuart spotted a mud hut with something on top of it. "Is that a satellite dish?"

Babauta answered, "Yup! Da tings all over da place. No electric out here. Hajjis running everything with gas generators."

Vasquez grinned. "We call 'em high tech red necks!"

The patrol entered Tuz. The roadside holes were gone. No bombs. Stuart breathed a little easier.

The streets were strewn with trash and dotted with stray dogs running in all directions. At one point, the group's progress was slowed by a wandering donkey in the middle of the road.

They drove by an empty building sprayed with graffiti that read 'Saddam is a jock off.'

Jock off? Stuart laughed.

They passed the huge mosque that was the site of the car bomb attack days before. Stuart marveled at its scale and beauty. He'd barely noticed the building the last time he was there. All along the top of the structure's terra cotta walls was a row of bright blue panels, each trimmed in gold and emblazoned with one of Islam's ninety-nine names of Allah.

Near the top of the tallest minaret, Stuart spotted a large set of loudspeakers that broadcast the five calls to prayer each day.

A left turn took them into the market section of town. It was a beehive of activity. Stuart guessed that this part of town had changed little over the last thousand years. Street vendors peddled their wares under multi-colored awnings as shoppers searched among them for the best bargains. If not for the cars lining the streets, it could have been a market place in ancient times.

Stuart was surprised by the friendly reception he received in Tuz. Parents smiled as children ran from their homes to wave at the American Humvees and give them the thumbs up as they passed. Their reactions to the sound of the Humvees reminded Stuart of American kids' reactions to the sound of an ice cream truck.

The children were beautiful. Stuart was surprised by the variety of eye colors, hair colors, and skin tones. In the Kurdish part of town, he saw many children with blonde hair and blue or green eyes. There were even some with hair red as fire.

The crowd of youngsters following the patrol grew larger. There was a commotion at the rear of the convoy. Stuart craned his neck but couldn't see what was happening.

Stuart tapped Babauta on the shoulder. "What's going on back there?"

"Kids poor. Barely having clothes. Most not having shoes. Not even knowing what toys are."

"What's that got to do with what's going on behind us?"

"Folks back home hearing about da kids. Dey sending toys and candy for 'em. Da last vehicle tossing 'em to da boys 'n girls we go by. Then dey not running between Humvees 'n getting run over."

Stuart thought the affluent residential areas of Tuz resembled some poor neighborhoods in Los Angeles, except these had narrower streets, donkey carts, and animal carcasses hung up and butchered in the open air.

Stuart was enthralled by the scenes passing his window. The bullet-proof glass separating him from the vistas scrolling by created a sense of detachment that made it seem almost as if he were watching a television documentary.

The patrol finally arrived at the Iraqi Police headquarters. It was like a small fort. The compound consisted of a large three-story cinder block building and courtyard surrounded by fifteen foot high cement walls, interrupted by two heavily guarded gates on the northern and eastern sides.

The courtyard filled with Iraqi police as they pulled in. Allen said to Stuart, "It's show time, Doc. I hope you're ready."

Stuart's insides turned to water.

11

The police chief, Hagir, stood in the courtyard as the Humvees came to a halt. He was middle aged and short, even by Iraqi standards. He wore the navy slacks and sky blue button down shirt of the Iraqi police. The man's lean face, which sported the standard Iraqi mustache, was hard with sharp, hawk-like features and crowned by a head of thinning salt and pepper hair. His sinewy frame looked to be all muscle, bone, and gristle. The lawman had the appearance of one tempered and beaten by a hard life. He looked tough as iron. Stuart could tell by the submissive demeanor of the subordinates at his side, the chief was not to be taken lightly.

Hagir shook Stuart's hand and said in near perfect English, "It is a pleasure to meet you, Doctor Knight." He then embraced Allen. "Good to see you my friend." He motioned them to the front door. "Please. Come in. We will see to your men."

The chief gave Stuart a tour of the building. Stuart peered around the gloomy interior as Hagir proudly led him through. The entire facility was in extreme disrepair.

Stuart mentally checked off every custom and courtesy from his state department brochure. It was easy for an outsider to violate the region's rigid formalities and accidentally offend his host.

The first stop was Hagir's office in the center of the bottom floor. It was small, worn, and sparsely furnished but clean. Allen was already there waiting there for them.

After seating his guests in two threadbare upholstered chairs, the chief sat at his desk. He opened a mini-fridge and pulled out two cans of cold soda.

"Something to drink?"

"Thank you." Stuart took one. Allen took the other.

"Doctor Knight, Colonel Hagir is a fascinating man." Allen made sure to call Stuart 'Doctor' to bolster the newcomer's credibility in Iraqi eyes. "The colonel is too modest to mention it, but he's a hero. He fought against Saddam Hussein as a leader in Peshmerga – Kurdish resistance."

"You fought Hussein?"

The chief nodded. "Yes. I was with Peshmerga for twenty years."

Stuart said, "I've never heard of Peshmerga."

"We Kurds have no country, but we have an army. Peshmerga was formed eighty years ago to defend our people. For years, we were all that stood between the Kurds and death at the hands of one dictator or another. Saddam tried for 25 years but could never defeat us." He smiled. "Peshmerga are fierce fighters."

"How did you come to be the chief of the Tuz police?"

"When the Americans came to Iraq, many in Peshmerga worked with them. We were hunted like animals for decades. Saddam drove us from our homes and butchered our families." The grizzled veteran's eyes moistened. "We all lost someone – parents, wives…" He swallowed hard and continued with difficulty, "And, for some… our children."

The cloud passed from his countenance as quickly as it had appeared. The old warrior regained his iron façade. "When you came, it was the first time in many years we tasted freedom. We no longer feared being shot like dogs or murdered by poison gas. Thanks to America, we Kurds are human beings again. And soon, we will have a country of our own."

Stuart took a drink from his soda. The beverage felt cool going down. "Has Peshmerga disbanded now that Saddam is gone?"

The chief shook his head. "No, Peshmerga is big as ever. Tuz is on the southwestern border of Kurdistan. Iraqi forces have no jurisdiction north or east of here. Kurdistan is policed by Peshmerga alone."

Allen asked, "Do you have any information about the car bomb in Tuz?"

Hagir shook his head. "No, my friend. We have heard nothing." He sighed. "It has made my job very difficult. Several Kurds were killed in the attack. They blame the Arabs, of course. I fear we will be unable to keep them in check if this is not stopped. We are on the verge of civil war."

"What about Al-Khayal?"

"Again, nothing. No one will talk. The people fear him more than they fear us."

"I saw him. He was on a cell phone just before the car bomb went off."

"Many Iraqis have cell phones. How can you be certain it was him?"

"It was him. I know it was him. He has a scarred face and one eye. I'd like to give your men some sketches of him so you can help bring him in."

Hagir smiled. "Of course."

A junior officer entered the room, saluted and reported quickly in Kurdish. The chief frowned and nodded curtly saying, "*Zurbash.*"

He stood, placing his right hand over his heart. "Please excuse me. Stay as long as you like. I must go now." He grabbed a cricket bat and followed his subordinate out the door.

Stuart asked Allen, "What was that about? I don't speak Kurdish."

Allen opened his soda and took a swig. "Neither do I, but, judging by the cricket bat, I'd say Hagir's guys caught a gang of kidnappers. They've been after the bastards for weeks. Those animals kidnapped the wife and five-year-old daughter of one of his men. They raped both of them, killed the mother, and cut the little girls legs off."

Stuart gasped. "Good Lord!"

"Hagir will make sure the bastards get what they deserve. He'll give 'em justice – Iraqi style."

Stuart wanted to protest, but a part of him – a bigger part than he wanted to admit – agreed with the captain.

Allen got to his feet. "Follow me."

They climbed the stairs to the roof. Allen was slowed by his fake leg. "You're gonna like this," Allen said as they crested the uppermost step.

"Wow!" Stuart said as Tuz spread out in a panoramic vista before him. He pulled a digital camera from his pocket. Again, he felt as if he were watching a movie. The muted palette of closely packed sand-colored houses was interrupted sporadically by brightly colored flags and ornate Persian rugs hung over garden walls.

To the south was a green area full of palm trees. It reminded Stuart of Central Park surrounded on all sides by a sprawling city. To his northeast was the tall ridgeline of a nearby mountain range. The bare mountains were the same brown hue as the buildings.

Below, the town people came and went on their daily business. The alien scene awakened Stuart's sense of adventure once again.

The noon call to prayer sounded. Chants washed over the town from the minarets of countless mosques. The voices intermingled as they echoed through the streets below in a ghostly chorus.

Stuart had never felt so windswept and daring. It was intoxicating. He turned to Allen. "This feels just like-"

"An Indiana Jones movie?" Allen finished the sentence.

"Yeah."

They sat in silence – spellbound by the sublime, exotic beauty of the landscape below.

Allen turned to Stuart. "What the hell do you hope to find here?"

"I'll know it when I find it."

"Babauta said you have a kid."

"Rachel. She's five. You?"

Allen nodded. "Little Jake. He's three. He and my wife, Emily, are home in Tennessee."

"Don't you miss them?"

"Of course I do."

Stuart asked, "Then why are you here? You could've gone home, but you volunteered just like me. What do *you* hope to find?"

"Justice."

"Why you?"

"You think anybody else is gonna do anything? No, Al-Khayal won't stop. My guys'll just keep dying. *I* have to end this."

"I can't believe you're willing to risk so much for that."

"That's pretty ballsy comin' from a guy risking it all to dig for trinkets in the sand."

Stuart glanced at Allen's leg. "Is this really just about your men?" He turned his attention to a boy riding a donkey laden with bundles of kindling. "I heard about what happened. I can't blame you for wanting revenge. I would too, but at what price? How far is too far?"

There was no reply.

Stuart looked around. "Captain?"

Allen was gone.

12

Hadi was in the cave again. It was completely dark. He couldn't see, but he sensed he wasn't alone. The walls echoed with the sound of his feet shuffling on the sandy floor as he groped in vain for walls that weren't there. He turned on his father's flashlight, but the ravenous darkness consumed the light until it disappeared, leaving him blind again. A voice called his name. It was only a whisper, but it was cruel and cold. It called again. He covered his ears. It didn't help. It was in his head.

Two dots of light grew from the gloom. Dim at first, they grew brighter and brighter into red-hot embers. Hadi knew what they were. He felt the ancient eyes look into him, searching his soul.

"*Haaaaadi*," the voice hissed again.

The boy shut his eyes and screamed, "No!"

Hadi opened his eyes to see the sun's first rays stretch across Tuz below him. He usually enjoyed sleeping under the stars, but not this time. He watched until the last star disappeared from the sky – erased by the light of a new day. He was aware of everything around him – the smell of fresh spices and bread from the market place, the sound of stray dogs fighting over scraps of food, the sight of vultures gliding through the cloudless sky, the feel of the morning breeze on his face. He closed his eyes, trying to remember it all. He hoped his plan would work, but knew in his heart he was likely doomed.

I will die today.

In spite of his fear, Hadi was resolved to follow through with his decision. He steeled himself for the trip to Faisal's shop.

Hadi stood and shouldered his bag, feeling the weight of the statue. He set out at a slow pace. He was determined to face his fate like a man, but he wasn't in a hurry.

*****

Stuart returned to the courtyard where the Humvees were parked. Allen was already there.

The captain summoned Hagir's second in command. An Iraqi major trotted into the courtyard and stopped in front of him with a sharp salute.

Allen said to the policeman, "We're conducting a foot patrol through the market district. I'd like some of your men to go along to help spread the word about Al-Khayal's description. I prefer Lieutenant Hussein."

The Iraqi saluted. "Of course, Captain. I will send Lieutenant Hussein and five officers with you."

"Good. We leave in five minutes."

Stuart opened a bottled water and said to Babauta who was checking their vehicle's fluids, "Five minutes isn't much notice. Don't we trust our allies?"

"Iraqi Security Forces corrupt. Moles all over. We being tight lipped. Not giving much notice. Dey understanding."

Lieutenant Hussein reported to Captain Allen. The officer was in his mid-twenties and in excellent physical condition. His uniform was immaculate with shoes highly shined. His mustache, jet black hair, and sharp features made the lieutenant resemble a younger version of his chief.

Babauta gave Stuart some background on the young officer. "Hussein being chief's best officer. Hagir loving like son. Dat surprising cuz Hagir being a Kurd and Hussein Arab."

"That *is* surprising."

"Hussein's uncle was police chief in Sulayman Bak. Arab town to south. Murdered by insurgents tree months ago. Hussein taking in uncle's wife and kids. Poor guy barely making enough to feed 'em."

"Has it affected his performance?"

"After uncle dying, he wearing bulletproof vest all da time."

Allen called to Babauta and spread a map over the front of their Humvee. "I'll lead the foot patrol. You and the Humvees stand by in case we run into trouble."

The sergeant asked, "How many men you taking?"

"Five of our guys, six Iraqis, and Doctor Knight. That makes 13 counting me."

Allen traced a path on the map. "This is our route. Should take two to three hours. Any trouble will likely come from snipers on rooftops or upper floor windows." He tapped a spot in a dead-end alley in the merchant district with his finger. "Here's the objective. Vacant storehouse. We have intel that Al-Khayal's boys are building another car bomb there." He folded the map and shoved it into his cargo pocket. "The marketplace is jumping this time of day. The crowd could cause problems if we have trouble."

"Iraqis knowing about target?"

"No. We'll tell 'em when we get there. They think it's just a P.R. patrol."

"Good." The sergeant furled his brow. "We reaching you on most of route. Few choke points concerning me. How you signaling us if you losing radio contact?"

The captain pulled a red flare from his cargo pocket. "I'll fire this off. Post a man on the roof of the police station. He can spot the signal easily from there."

"Be knowing dat if you calling, we coming with sharp teeth."

"I'd be disappointed by anything less." The captain left to gather his patrol.

After the mission brief, rehearsal, and weapons, equipment, and ammunition checks, they were ready to go.

Allen pulled Stuart aside. "There are only two things to remember: Stay alert and stay close to me. Got it?"

"Got it."

The men assembled and moved out toward the market district.

Stuart saw two Iraqi patrol members putting on ski masks. He asked a soldier, "What are they doing?"

"So they won't be recognized by insurgents. They're afraid of reprisals."

"And for good reason considering what I heard at the station." Stuart took a picture of one of the hooded men. "Still, it is a little creepy."

The soldier smiled. "Yeah. One time I emailed a picture to my wife with one of 'em behind me wearing a ski mask and carrying an AK74. She freaked out when she saw it."

A small roadside stand sat on the outskirts of the market district. It offered live chickens. The proprietor was proud of his poultry. He pulled one of them out of a wire cage and held it up for Stuart to take a picture.

The cinder block buildings on each of the narrow street were two and three stories high. Power lines and cords with decorative multicolored streamers and small flags, the type normally adorning a car lot, criss-crossed above the crowded street.

Allen signaled to his men to watch the upper floors for snipers.

The trash strewn street was dotted with vendor carts selling all types of wares: candy, vegetables, cheap plastic trinkets, fresh fish, and prescription narcotics, to name a few.

Piles of empty cardboard boxes littered the street in every direction. Papers, empty plastic bottles, and aluminum cans were everywhere.

A trench of dark liquid ran between the sidewalk and the road.

Stuart pointed to the trench and asked the soldier next to him, "Is this what I think it is?"

The soldier nodded. "Better watch your step around here, sir."

Stuart noticed that Allen's limp was getting worse. "How's the leg?"

"I'll live."

Stuart wiped his brow with his sleeve, "I'm burning up. What'll you do this summer when it hits 150 degrees?"

"Drink water and think cool thoughts."

The crowd thickened as the patrol went deeper in. The sound of car horns and foreign tongues became the tune to which they marched.

As he walked from one block to another, Stuart realized this market district was organized according to the products sold in each section. To his rear was the clothing street. Ahead, Stuart saw the produce street.

There were potatoes, tomatoes, onions, olives, and spices. Most were in large, open baskets in storefronts. As he passed one shop, the smell of fresh curry filled his nostrils.

It's like walking back in time.

Stuart watched the soldiers in their heavy helmets and armor. He imagined the Roman legionaries of Trajan's Mesopotamian expedition two thousand years before. That Iraqi campaign was a failure. He wondered how history would judge this one.

Stuart carefully stepped over a fly infested pile of trash. A few paces later, he bumped into a table, knocking some shoes off. He replaced them and apologized to the shopkeeper.

A group of boys approached. They asked for chewing gum, candy, and whatever else the soldiers carried. The men gave what they had and the youths tagged along.

Allen pointed to the children, "They're our best hope for success here."

Stuart took some pictures of them. "The kids?"

"We can make an impression on these kids. Over half the population of Iraq is fifteen or younger. We gotta reach 'em while they're young. We can't change a 25 year old insurgent's mind." He pointed to the youths. "But we can reach them."

One of the soldiers knelt to play with the children.

Allen said, "Kids are a good barometer of a neighborhood."

"How so?" Stuart took more pictures of the soldier and children playing.

"Adults put up a false front. Kids don't. They reflect their parents' true feelings. If they're friendly like these, you're pretty safe. If they stand and stare at you like *The Children of the Corn*, their parents don't like you. Then there's the worst case."

Stuart stopped snapping photos. "Worst case?"

"No kids at all. There's only one thing to do then."

"What's that?"

"Get the hell out of Dodge."

The children moved on. The squad made a left turn and entered the meat market. A man crouched over a goat's severed head hacking the horns off with a hatchet. More goat heads lined the ground next to him. The animals' hides were stacked in a pile a few feet away. The stench was overpowering. Flies were everywhere.

Stuart began snapping pictures again. "You don't see *that* every day."

"You do here."

A butcher saw Stuart taking photos. He grabbed a sheep from his shop and ran to the door holding up the carcass for Stuart.

A soldier pulled the doorway curtain aside for an Iraqi woman to enter. She smiled at the trooper as she passed, but her husband shot the soldier a hateful look and slapped his wife.

Stuart saw the guilt and anger in the young soldier's face.

A different world.

Allen said, "Be careful who you take pictures of here. The men are jealous, especially the Shiites."

"I see what you mean."

Stuart stowed his camera and the patrol moved on. They took a left at the furniture market. At the end of this street, they made another turn.

Stuart passed another pile of foul-smelling garbage. He wrinkled his nose. "It's a miracle there isn't a cholera epidemic here."

A nearby sergeant scanned the rooftops as he replied, "These people have no concept of bacteria, viruses, and the like. They can't believe something so small could hurt 'em. We had a heck of a time with the food at the hajji shop on the base. Still beats the mess hall though."

Allen added, "They have to pull themselves out of the dark ages before they can ever know the light of freedom. That's our mission. But we can't do it until we cut out the cancers like Al-Khayal. Then, we'll be able help Iraq."

"You think that's possible?"

"We have to try," Allen said before moving to the front of the formation.

Stuart asked the sergeant, "What if they don't want to change?"

"These are good people if you get to know 'em. They're smart. Most of 'em speak at least two languages. They're like us in a lot of ways. We'd be the same if we'd been born in their shoes."

Stuart saw an Iraqi man talking on a mobile phone. "They're making progress. I see a lot of cell phones here."

The soldier nodded. "The Iraqis know their lives are shit. They see American television and want our lifestyle – at least the lifestyle they *think* we have. They're convinced we all drive luxury cars and have beach houses in Malibu."

Stuart pointed at the trash around them. "Then why don't they do something about this?"

"They figure they can survive without clean water, electricity, and sanitation because they've always done without it. They want sexy stuff like cell phones, satellite TV, and nice cars. It's like eating the icing without the cake."

Stuart took a chance. "What do you think about the war?"

"I think it's bullshit. We shouldn't even be here."

"I thought you guys were all in favor of it."

"Nope. I think it's one huge-ass mistake. Hell, I'm a democrat. I didn't even vote for Bush."

"Then why are you here?"

He pointed to his fellow soldiers. "I believe in them."

13

The group reached another intersection and entered the construction market. Across the street was a storage yard full of the thin wooden beams used to make roofs for houses. On Stuart's side of the street was a paint store.

The sergeant called to Stuart, "This is my department!"

"How's that?"

The sergeant smiled. "I work at a Lowe's back home!"

Stuart remembered that none of these men were fulltime soldiers. It was hard to picture them as plumbers, plant workers, teachers, and mechanics.

Construction supply stores soon gave way to electronics shops full of televisions, radios, and satellite dishes.

Stuart's sense of adventure began to wilt under searing sun and heavy body armor. He had forgotten to drink water. He grabbed his canteen and gulped down several mouths full.

The sergeant nodded at a painting in a shop window. The image was of an ancient warrior in full armor. "I've got to hand it to these folks. They know their history better than we know ours."

"History is all they have."

"Say again?"

"Like you said, the Iraqis know their lives are shit. It's made worse by the knowledge of their ancestors' greatness. This is the cradle of civilization: the land of the Babylonians and the Assyrians. They once ruled the known world. While our ancestors were beating each other with clubs in the Dark Ages, theirs were studying medicine, mathematics, and astronomy. Algebra was invented just south of here in Baghdad. The word 'algebra' is Arabic, just like *Al*-Qaeda or *Al*-Jazeera. Our number system is composed of *Arabic* numerals. They've gone from being the most advanced civilization in the world to this." He gestured to the piles of filth around them.

The sergeant watched a woman dig through one of the piles for food. "Long way to fall."

"That's why an Iraqi can speak of an event that occurred a thousand years ago as if it happened yesterday. This long cultural memory means grudges are held for generations. The whole society is like a middle-aged guy that hit the game winning home run in high school and still lives in that moment because he hasn't done anything to top it since. He spends the rest of his life living in the shadow of his former self, haunted by the ghost of bygone glory. Even Saddam Hussein wasn't immune. During his regime, he spent much of his time rebuilding Nebakanezer's palace in Babylon as well as other ancient sites around Iraq. He claimed to be a direct descendant of Nebakanezer himself."

"So, basically, the Iraqis are haunted by the ghosts of Babylon."

"In a nutshell, yes."

Stuart was continually surprised by the warm reception the Iraqis gave the patrol. Everywhere they went, people waved and greeted the Americans cordially. One shop owner even gave them candy as they walked by. But Stuart sensed that all was not as well as it seemed.

There was an underlying disquiet that couldn't be denied. Easy smiles and welcoming gestures were betrayed by eyes filled with foreboding. Whether it was Anti-American sentiment, fear of insurgent attacks, or the Kurdish-Arab tension, he didn't know. But, given the area's history, Stuart did know each was enough to turn the place into a pressure cooker ready to blow.

They turned onto a street so narrow it made the buildings on each side seem taller than they were. Large canvases stretched across the alley overhead, providing shade for the customers and merchants.

Allen called to the group, "We'll conduct a short halt here. Keep your eyes open."

Feeling at ease, Stuart set out to explore the shops and meet the locals.

Allen warned the professor, "Stay close. Remember, this is a war zone."

*****

Hadi stood tall as he marched into Faisal's shop.

"I knew you would come." Faisal's lips parted in a sinister grin. A gold tooth gleamed in a sliver of sunlight that penetrated the interior of the store. The shaft of radiance illuminated particles of dust dancing around the man's head.

To Hadi, the floating specks looked like the souls of a thousand victims tethered to a demon by some unholy bond. For the first time, he saw Faisal for what he really was.

He took the bag containing the statue and held it out to the monster.

Faisal's hand passed over the bag and grabbed Hadi's arm. "It is not that easy, boy. I will make you pay." He slapped Hadi hard across the face.

*****

Hadi's father thought of his son as he worked in his barley field. He hadn't seen the boy since the confrontation with Faisal. He had no idea what Hadi had done to the Arab. He only knew that his son had brought shame upon the family.

He had tried to turn the boy from Faisal's path, but Hadi would not listen. The temptation was too much for his son to resist. The stubborn youth would pay for his choice.

The farmer shrugged and dug into the soil. This was the only end his son could have expected.

He hoped Hadi could make amends before he died. Then, at least the family wouldn't lose face.

He loved his son, but Allah could give him another. Children were born every day and didn't cost a dinar. A destroyed reputation, on the other hand, would last a lifetime.

Life was cheap in this part of the world – even the life of one's own child.

*****

During the halt, Stuart walked down the street, admiring the merchandise. A shop three doors down caught his eye. Its facade was decorated with brightly colored Persian rugs. A rack in the front window was adorned with antiquities. Stuart knew they were probably counterfeits, but it was worth a look. Even if they were, he wouldn't mind shopping for an authentic, hand-made Persian carpet. He could get one here for a fraction of the cost in America.

Stuart glanced back. The captain was busy talking on the radio to the Humvees.

This'll just take a minute. Stuart ducked into the little shop.

*****

"Roger Raider Two Alpha. Moving to target. Raider Two out." Captain Allen released the hand mic and waved Lieutenant Hussein over. "Change of mission. You and your guys provide an outer cordon. My team and I are going after a target."

"Yes Captain."

Allen and his men moved quickly into position outside the storehouse.

*****

The interior of the shop was hot and musty. Stuart saw instantly that the trinkets were fakes, but the carpets were beautiful. He went further in to look at more.

"Hello?" Stuart didn't see anyone at first. Then he heard a voice coming from a room in the back. He followed the voice to find a heavy set man standing over a crying, hazel-eyed boy.

*****

The breach team was in place. The assault team was coiled feet away, ready to strike. All was ready. Allen gave a nod.

"Flash out!" The breach team smashed in the door and tossed in a flash-bang grenade. Its deafening report signaled the assault team to storm the building. The three man group rushed into the dark portal with weapons raised. Allen entered right behind them.

*****

Faisal backhanded the boy savagely. Hadi screamed, but then froze with fear as Faisal reached for the pistol tucked in the small of his back.

The Arab growled, "Where is the cave?"

*****

"Right clear!"

"Left clear!"

"Center clear!"

The room was empty.

Allen and his men rapidly searched the rest of the building. Nothing.

A sergeant reported to Allen, "Looks like a big time operation. We got tire tracks, welding residue, metal shavings, and a workbench upstairs covered with wire clippings and solder. Equipment's all gone, though. This is all we found." He handed the captain the guts from a cell phone. "Looks like we just missed 'em. They were in a hurry, but they cleaned the place pretty good, sir."

"Shit!" Allen smashed the component against the wall. "They knew we were coming before we left the police station."

"What do you wanna do, sir."

"Nothing we can do here. Let's go."

Allen's team met up with Hussein and his men outside.

The lieutenant asked, "Did you find what you were looking for, Captain?"

"No. Gather your men. We're going back to the station." He looked around. "Where the hell's Knight?"

*****

Stuart spoke loudly in Arabic. "*Salaam!*"

Faisal spun round — shocked to see an America in a navy blue Kevlar helmet and body armor. His hand moved away from his pistol as he looked the newcomer up and down. "Who are you? What do you want?"

The boy babbled excitedly to Stuart in a language he couldn't understand. Stuart addressed the man in broken Arabic. "Why you hit the boy?"

"He is my son. It is not your business."

The boy was desperate. He cried frantically as he tried to crawl to Stuart.

Faisal shoved him into the corner and snarled at the American, "We're closed! Come back tomorrow!"

Allen entered the shop with Lieutenant Hussein. "What the hell's goin' on in here?"

When Hadi saw the tall American officer enter the building, he had an idea. He grabbed his bag from the floor next to Faisal and pulled out the statue. He held it up and started yelling, "Thief! The man is a thief!"

Allen asked Hussein, "What are they saying?" His eyes and rifle were both trained on Faisal and the boy. He didn't know which, if either of them, had hostile intentions. He doubted it was the boy.

"The man is telling us to leave. The boy says the man is a thief."

Stuart looked down at Hadi. The youth's face was streaked with dirt and tears. He waved something excitedly as he screamed.

Stuart glanced at the boy's hands. *What's that?*

He knelt to calm the boy and get a closer look at the object in his hands. Recognition flashed in Stuart's eyes. He gently removed the artifact from the child's quivering grasp.

Faisal reached to push Stuart away but was stopped cold by Allen's palm in his chest.

The Arab stumbled backward as Hadi latched onto Stuart's leg.

Allen kept his weapon aimed at the portly shopkeeper and told Hussein. "Watch the kid. I'll cover fat boy!"

He snapped at Stuart. "What the hell's goin' on here?"

Stuart sputtered – addled by the sudden, violent confrontation. "I don't, uh, I'm not certain…"

Jake barked, "Spit it out!"

Stuart's mouth went dry. He could barely speak. "I think he's the boy's father."

"Then why aren't they speaking the same language?"

Hussein answered. "He is Arab. The boy is a Kurd. He cannot be the child's father."

14

Hadi still clung to Stuart's leg, but the academic barely noticed him. His focus was on the statue in his hands. Stuart fondled it like a jeweler with a precious stone.

Stuart held up the artifact and spoke to Faisal. "Where did you get this?"

Faisal didn't answer.

Hussein asked, "What do you want to do, Captain?"

Allen eyed Faisal suspiciously. "No point in arresting this dirt bag. He hasn't done anything illegal that we know of."

"What about the boy?"

Stuart suggested, "We could bring him with us...For his safety."

Allen said, "He can come with us if he wants to." He told Hussein, "Get this guy's full name and verify it with paperwork from the shop."

Hadi stood and held Stuart's hand.

Stuart smiled. "I guess he's coming with us."

Allen looked Faisal in the eye and said to Hussein, "Tell him if he as much as farts upwind of me, I'll be back for him."

Allen told Stuart, "You watch the kid. Let's go."

They rejoined the patrol and the group wound its way back to the police station. Stuart barely looked up from the statue the entire time.

Allen asked, "Where's the kid?"

Stuart looked around. "He was right behind me." He scanned the formation and spotted Hadi walking next to one of the soldiers. "There he is!"

"I told you to watch the kid. Put that damn thing away"

Stuart waved Hadi to him. "I'd like him to stay on the base with us for a while. Just until we can find his parents. If this thing is authentic, we'll need to find out where he got it."

"We'll see."

Colonel Hagir greeted the patrol at the police station.

"Welcome back gentlemen! I hope all went well."

Allen shook the colonel's hand. "Not as well as I'd hoped. Thanks for your help, though."

"Think nothing of it." He looked down amusedly at Hadi, who hid behind Stuart's leg. "Doctor Knight, who is your little friend?"

"His name is Hadi. He was in trouble with a local merchant. We brought him along to keep him from getting hurt."

"He likes you," Hagir chuckled. "Doctor, I would be honored if you joined us for dinner."

Stuart glanced at Allen. The captain nodded. Turning down the invitation would have been an insult.

Stuart smiled. "The honor is mine, Colonel."

"Excellent! My men are excited to meet you. The food will be here soon."

Allen said to Hagir, "Colonel, could we discuss something in your office before the meal?"

"As you wish, Captain." The two walked into the police station.

Stuart went to his Humvee and found Hadi in the back seat, playing with a chem-light. The boy waved at him cheerfully.

Babauta tossed the child a chocolate Hooah Bar and said, "Cute kid. I never figuring you to take in strays."

Stuart shrugged. "Got a soft spot for kids I guess." He unconsciously gripped the bag containing the statue.

The islander laughed, "He sure making himself at home. Whatcha doing with him?"

"Captain Allen said he might be able to stay on the base for a while."

"Dat's good."

"Do you think he'll be alright out here while we eat with the colonel?"

"I ain't eating in dere."

"Why not?"

"Dis party for officers 'n VIP's. We not invited."

"Well, if you can't go, neither will I."

"Don't sweat it, Doc. Dey bringing us plates. I feeling sorry for you! You being center of attention in dere! At least we getting to eat in peace!"

Stuart smiled. "Good point."

Lieutenant Hussein arrived and saluted smartly. "Doctor Knight. I will escort you to dinner."

The lieutenant took him to a room on the ground floor which resembled a smaller version of Bernstein's operations center. The flaking, dingy walls were covered with maps. Workstations were interspersed along the sides. A long, folding table occupied the room's center. There were, as Stuart had learned to expect, plenty of plastic lawn chairs. Four men sat at the stations, listening to radios. Each wore a different uniform. They stood to attention as soon as the pair entered.

Hussein put the men at ease and waved his hand across the space. "This is the JCC."

"JCC?" Stuart asked.

The lieutenant bowed his head slightly and touched his chest. "I apologize. I assume too much. JCC stands for Joint Coordination Center. This is where representatives from our military, police, and emergency services work together with U.S. forces to coordinate their efforts. It ensures information is passed between all of these entities efficiently. It is our nerve center. It is also where we will be eating."

Hussein supervised the radio operators as they prepared the room for their guests, then shooed them out the door.

Captain Allen entered as Lieutenant Hussein left. He pulled Stuart aside and said quietly, "Be careful what you say in here. We don't know who we can trust."

"Babauta already filled me in."

"Good."

"What were you talking to Colonel Hagir about?"

A group of Iraqi officers entered the room.

Allen said to Stuart, "Just watch what you say."

Hagir entered and announced, "The food is here. Captain Allen has requested that his men in the courtyard be served first. Please make yourselves at home, my friends. We will eat soon."

Stuart followed Allen's lead and stacked his gear in the corner as the room filled with local dignitaries. When all the guests arrived, introductions were made all around. Everyone wanted to speak to Stuart. He felt like a celebrity. He tried to divide his attention without insulting anyone. He lost count of how many pictures the Iraqis took with him.

As was Iraqi custom, professional business waited until a personal rapport was established. All of the men passed around pictures of their children. Photos of wives were not shared. It was taboo.

Stuart took Rachel's picture from his wallet. It was the only one he had – taken two years ago when she was three. He thought of how he'd seen her only twice since then. Regret crept into his heart.

An Iraqi officer presented a picture of his young son to Stuart. The professor offered his in return.

The Iraqi was so taken with Rachel's likeness, he proposed an arranged marriage between her and his boy. Trying not to offend the man, Stuart declined, saying he couldn't bear her living so far away. He realized as he spoke that there was more truth in his words than he intended.

Stuart didn't feel like a VIP. His face was gritty and his clothes were covered with sweat and salt stains. He knew he reeked, but no one seemed to notice.

After a few more minutes of hectic but cordial conversation, the food arrived. Everyone was served a regional delicacy called kuzi which was sheep shoulder on a bed of rice. It was served with Iraqi baked beans. Stuart found them similar to the American version, but firmer with a strong tomato taste. There was a soup that tasted like beefy vegetable infused with exotic spices. Naan bread and vegetables were also served. Stuart thoroughly enjoyed the meal and the company.

Most of the Iraqis left after eating and chatting for a few more minutes.

Stuart looked for Allen, but the captain was gone again.

As the last dinner guest left, Lieutenant Hussein said to Stuart, "Captain Allen said to stay here until he gets back. I will stay with you. He won't be long."

The radio operators returned to the room and took their posts. The police station returned to business as usual.

Shadows grew slowly, creeping across the room as Stuart waited in the JCC with Hussein and the night crew.

Hussein looked at Stuart apprehensively. He started to speak, but stopped.

"What's on your mind?" Stuart asked.

"I have helped Americans for a long time, but I know nothing of your country. I have many questions."

"Ask away. I'll tell you all I can."

"America was born out of a revolution against the British, yes?"

"Yes."

"Then how can you be friends? Do they not seek to control you again?"

"No. We've helped each other for many years." Stuart interlocked his fingers to demonstrate the bond between the two nations. "The British are now our closest allies."

Hussein shook his head. "I do not think the Kurds and Arabs can ever be friends like this."

"I hope that's not the case."

Hussein changed the subject, "How are marriages arranged in America?"

Stuart smiled. "They're not."

"Then how does marriage happen? Who matches people together?"

"They match themselves. Men and women in America go on dates with different people until they meet the one that they want to marry."

"What are dates?"

"A date is when a man and a woman go someplace to get to know each other – usually some place like a movie theater or restaurant."

"Who goes with them to see that they don't….?"

"There are no chaperones. And sometimes they do…"

Hussein's jaw dropped at the scandalous revelation.

Stuart laughed.

The JCC radios hissed and popped in the background. A bored operator yawned as another lit a cigarette.

The lieutenant asked, "What about Hitler?"

"What about him?"

"He was a great leader, yes?"

Stuart thought a moment. "Yes, but he was also very evil."

"Tell me about this. Under Saddam, all we learned was that Hitler was a great man that fought the Jews. He wanted to be like him."

"Hitler *murdered* millions of innocent people."

Hussein shrugged. "But they were just Jews."

"They were people. He took them from their homes and murdered them. He was a mad man. He butchered them just to make Germany racially pure."

"That sounds like Saddam and the Kurds. He wanted to cleanse them from Iraq. Mosul, Tikrit, and Tuz were Kurdish before Saddam drove them out. He gave their houses and property to Arabs he had moved there from the south.

"He killed many Kurds, too. In 1988, he attacked the town of Halabja with poison gas. Five thousand Kurds died in a single morning. Colonel Hagir's family was killed there. He was in the mountains, fighting with Peshmerga when it happened. Today is the seventeenth anniversary of that day."

"Poor guy."

"When the Americans came and Saddam fell, the Kurds returned for their property. That is how Colonel Hagir came to Tuz. He was a leader in the Peshmerga forces that reclaimed this place."

"But Tuz is still half Arab."

"Yes. The Kurds' conquest is not finished. The Americans stopped them before they could take back all of their lands. So Tuz is divided."

A static filled voice reported in Arabic over the army radio. The operator responded in a robotic tone, then laid the mic back on the table.

Hussein leaned in and whispered reluctantly, "Do you have… magic in America?"

"We have illusion…sleight of hand. But they're just tricks."

Hussein shook his head. "No, Doctor. I am talking about *real* magic. Do you have *real* magic in America?"

"No. There's no such thing."

Hussein's voice quivered, "I believe in magic. I have seen it."

"Where?"

"It is very common here. It is used by the Shiite Sheiks – holy men. It came from India and spread across Iran. In Iraq, it is practiced most in the city of Najaf. I worked as a sheik's assistant there. That is where I saw the magic work."

Stuart was hooked. "What did you see?"

"The sheik takes money from customers in return for putting curses on people. He rearranges the words of the Koran on a piece of parchment. This is the price required by the djinn."

"Djinn?"

"They are evil spirits. They are invisible but are always moving among us like shadows, causing mischief. They are the djinn."

"Like demons?"

Hussein nodded.

So the genie in the lamp is really the demon in the lamp. I'll never see 'Aladdin' the same way again.

"How can a holy man converse with demons?"

"Not all sheiks do this. There are good ones and bad ones. Only the dark sheiks practice this magic."

"So, what did you see, exactly?"

"I was a scribe. The sheik would tell me what to write for each curse and then he would give it to the customer. He made people very sick. He could make their teeth fall out and worse. Some even died."

Stuart was captivated. "Tell me more."

"Time to go!" Allen appeared in the doorway.

Stuart and Hussein jumped. The bored Iraqis manning the JCC radios chuckled and went back to their duties.

Stuart gathered his things. Magic would have to wait.

15

Stuart and Allen walked to the courtyard. Allen called out to his men, "Mount up!"

Stuart asked, "What about Hadi?"

"Who?"

"The kid from the shop."

"What about him?"

"We can't just leave him."

"He's a kid, not a puppy."

"It'll just be until we can find his family. What if that shop owner comes looking for him?"

"The quarters next to yours in P-quad are empty. He can stay there for now, but you're responsible for him."

"Agreed."

Stuart and Babauta climbed into their Humvee. Hadi sat on a pile of gear between them. Half way back to Bernstein, the boy slid into Stuart's lap and fell asleep on his shoulder.

Gravel crunched and popped under their tires as they pulled into the quad. Babauta helped put the child to bed in the billet next to Stuart's.

After Hadi was settled, Stuart hurried to his quarters, locked the door, and seized the statuette from Hadi's bag.

He ran his hands over the black stone – still warm from the day's heat. He stared into its monstrous eyes.

What are you?

He eagerly eyed the characters etched around the base. Stuart didn't recognize the language. He grabbed a pencil and meticulously copied the inscription onto a notepad. It felt good. It felt right. For the first time in years, Stuart felt like an archaeologist.

*****

Captain Allen returned to his office. Al-Khayal had a mole – a damn good one. The spy had to be rooted out. He had to plug the leak.

Allen studied the maps and intel reports that covered the walls of his office. The answer was there – hidden somewhere in the mountain of data.

It was long past midnight when the base security radio crackled to life. It was the ground surveillance radar team. Their super sensitive set of electronic ears used pulsed Doppler radar to detect movement at long range. GSR could hear someone walking from 4 miles away.

They reported heavy vehicle and foot traffic in the same location of the decoy IED the day Stuart came to Bernstein.

The command center's crew knew the drill and put it into action. They launched the remote controlled Raven aerial surveillance vehicle to investigate the radar contact. It was hand-launched and equipped with a thermal camera that could broadcast real-time video to a flat-screen television in the command center.

Allen joined the men in the command center and watched the live feed from the Raven as it flew over the suspect site.

One of the night crew said, "Nobody there. Looks like a false alarm."

"Right there." Allen pointed at the screen to a shadow in the middle of the road intersection. "Look at this. It doesn't belong. Call up the quick reaction force to investigate."

"Yes, sir."

Allen asked, "Who's got QRF duty tonight?"

"Alpha Company, sir."

"Crumm's guys. Shit."

Sergeant Parson entered the command center and said to Allen, "I couldn't sleep. Thought I'd come by and see if you needed a hand."

Crumm's voice came over the radio. "We are unable to provide a reaction force. My men are tired and getting them up now would interfere with our rest plan."

"Why the hell is *he* up so late?" Allen grabbed the hand mic. "We have a possible contact at check point 13. If we don't check it out tonight, our guys could have a bad day tomorrow."

Sergeant Parson pulled a small flash drive from his pocket. He gave it to Vasquez, who was recording the night's events into the battalion duty log on a laptop computer. "Here. Record *every* detail. If the crap hits the fan, we're the first ones they'll come after. We ain't takin' the fall for somethin' that ain't our fault. Back up the log onto this stick. That way it can't be changed or 'accidentally' erased."

Allen keyed the handset again. "It's your job to provide the reaction force. You're supposed to have a platoon standing by, ready to roll in five minutes."

There was a long pause before Crumm finally responded, "Fine. I'll tell my guys to check it out."

Allen gave the mic back to the radio operator and limped to the door. "I'm going to get some sleep. Call me if they find anything."

*****

Stuart still sat hunched in his chair, studying the sculpture. His head ached and he was seeing double. He yawned and stretched his tired back.

I need some air.

Stuart stepped outside. It was even hotter. He looked up. A million stars dotted the moonless sky. The quad was so black, Stuart couldn't see his hand in front of his face.

He thought he detected a faint whisper just on the edge of hearing. It called his name. Stuart shivered as a chill crept into his bones in spite of the night's warmth.

He spotted something – a pair of glowing eyes staring back from the gloom.

Stuart rubbed his own strained eyes, peering into the pitch as he eased back toward his billet door.

"Hello? Who's there?"

The glow returned, but wasn't a pair of eyes. It was a single dot of amber phosphorescence.

The ball grew brighter and Stuart thought he saw a face revealed in its brilliance. He reached a hand into his room and turned on his porch light.

The night hungrily consumed the lamp's feeble effort, but it was just bright enough for Stuart to make out the silhouette of a man smoking outside a nearby housing unit.

Stuart waved. "Hello there. You gave me quite a scare."

The man said nothing.

As his eyes adjusted, Stuart saw the shadow in more detail. He was Iraqi. Deep set eyes stared at the American silently from under a heavy brow. A thick, dark beard hid most of the swarthy stranger's face. He was dressed in black from head to foot.

Stuart tried again. "Hi! Do you speak English? Arab? Salaam!"

The enigmatic figure simply slid back into the darkness.

The professor warily returned to his quarters and locked the door. He gripped the statue and went back to work, stopping every so often to peek apprehensively out the window.

16

Stuart was surrounded by absolute darkness. He had no idea where he was. He called out, but the only answer was his own echo bouncing back from the gloom. He reached out, but felt no walls.

A light appeared, but Stuart couldn't tell what it was. It hid behind a wall of swirling black smoke. He started to reach through it, but stopped short. Something told him not to.

But something else spurred him on – the promise of fame, wealth, and glory. The thing beyond the dark cloud – whatever it was – promised to fulfill his wildest dreams.

Stuart couldn't resist. A finger pierced the fog. It was so cold, his hand went numb. He withdrew, but the darkness clung to him like tar. It began to spread. It engulfed his hand and climbed his arm. He couldn't shake it off. It was at his shoulder now. He could barely breathe. His neck and chest came next. He fell to the ground. He couldn't move. He screamed as the icy pitch covered his face.

Stuart jerked awake. It was early morning. He was slumped over his desk, still clutching the idol. He rubbed his bloodshot eyes and put the statue back in its bag. Stiff joints popped as he stood and stretched his aching limbs.

Stuart scanned his Spartan surroundings. The floor was gritty beneath his feet. The room felt like an oven in spite of the air conditioner. His gear was covered in sand.

"I'm getting too old for this shit."

His bladder felt like it was about to explode. He spotted one boot by his chair. After searching for what seemed an eternity, he found the other under his duffel. He quickly checked them for scorpions just like the pamphlet said to do, then slipped them on and jogged to the latrine.

On his way back, he spotted Babauta in the middle of the quad. The islander was stripped to the waist. For the first time, Stuart saw the extent of the sergeant's tattoos. The thick, squiggly patterns covered his entire upper body.

Babauta assumed a menacing stance and pulled his father's knife from its sheath. Stuart took a step back. Then it began.

The sergeant moved his hands sharply and stomped in rhythm to an ancient Polynesian chant. Babauta's tongue darted in and out as he blared his eyes and slashed with the ancestral blade.

A voice behind Stuart said, "Cap'n Allen wants to see you ASAP." The professor jumped.

"Sorry, Doc. Didn't mean to scare ya." Sergeant Parson said as he watched Babauta, "What's he doin'?"

"The Haka, I think."

The tattooed sergeant was covered in sweat. His massive muscles rippled as he energetically continued his chant.

"What the heck's a Haka?"

Stuart replied, "Mauri war chant. Does he do it often?"

"Nope. This is the first I've seen."

Babauta roared a fierce war cry, then it was done. He sheathed the knife and walked to Stuart.

The islander handed Stuart his father's blade. "Ancestors coming to me in dream. Dey saying give to you for protection."

Stuart accepted the gift and asked, "Protection from what?"

"Atua." Babauta offered a blessing in his native tongue and left.

Parson said, "The demon."

"You speak Mauri?" Stuart asked.

"No."

"Then how did you kno-"

"There's a presence here. It's old...real old. It's strong, too. And it's after you, Doc. I see it all around you like a swarm of flies."

Stuart chuckled, "I'll take my chances."

"You won't be laughin' long. Once evil gets a hold of your soul, it don't let go. I don't know what you're messin' with, but you best be careful."

Stuart's smile dimmed, "I don't believe in that stuff."

"It's like steppin' in dog crap. It'll get all over you whether you believe in it or not. How ya been sleepin'. Had any nightmares lately?"

Stuart said uncomfortably, "You said Captain Allen wanted to see me. Did he say why?"

"Nope." The veteran added, "But I wouldn't keep him waitin' if I was you."

*****

Stuart entered Allen's office a few minutes later. The captain met him with a contemptuous gaze and barked, "Sit!"

Stuart considered protesting, but then thought better of it.

"What the hell happened in the carpet shop yesterday?"

"I don't know. I guess I just froze."

"Your application to the State Department says you speak Arabic fluently. Do you?"

"I read it fluently."

"That's not what I asked."

"I'm just a little rusty."

"Liar!" He put a finger in Stuart's chest. "I'll be damned if I let you get my men killed just to pad your fuckin' resume."

A voice called out from the operations center next door, "IED located near Check Point 13! Artillery round on the side of the road!"

Allen growled at Stuart, "Don't move."

The captain entered the command center and took charge. "That's the same spot as last night. Did Crumm's guys report anything there?"

A soldier typing at the laptop scanned the duty log. "No, sir."

"Okay, establish a perimeter four hundred meters on each side of the round. Tell 'em to scan around their vehicles for secondary devices and report when finished. Call Boomer. Tell him we've got business. Then get an escort platoon here ASAP."

The radio operator hung up the land line. "Boomer's on his way, sir."

Tense moments passed before the patrol leader's next report. "Perimeter set. Scan complete. No other devices found."

The voices on the radios told Allen as much about the situation on the ground as the content of their reports. Everyone was calm. So far, so good.

Boomer entered the operations center. "What's up?"

R.A. MATHIS

Allen pointed to the wall map. "Artillery round in the road at check point 13."

"Do they see any wires or antennas?"

"No. Just the shell."

Boomer looked uneasy. The expert had disabled nearly a hundred explosive devices during his tour. He was still alive because he always listened to his gut. It was never wrong.

Allen noticed his disquiet and asked, "You okay?"

Boomer nodded. "Yeah. Good to go."

"Your escort platoon is on its way. The patrol on the ground is equipped with a Warlock. It'll jam any radio signals, so you shouldn't have to worry about remote detonation devices."

"Good to know."

Allen grabbed his body armor. "I'm going with you." He yelled to Stuart, "Get your shit, professor! It's time to earn your pay!"

*****

They arrived at the scene twenty minutes later. The flat, featureless landscape that greeted them was a familiar sight.

Boomer scanned the few scattered rises in the tabletop terrain with a seasoned eye. Harvest time was near. In the huts and swaying fields, all he could see were hiding places for insurgents. Looking south, he surveyed the T-shaped crossroads the battalion called checkpoint 13. He wondered if his nemesis was watching.

He raised a pair of binoculars and examined the artillery round. He couldn't see a timer or trigger device. The robot could have told him for sure, but it was gone – blown to bits by the IED in Tuz.

The shell looked innocent enough from where Boomer stood – battlefield flotsam. A common sight. Iraq was littered with stray munitions.

Boomer looked over the fields again and saw nothing but barley swaying in the morning breeze.

He reached for his tool belt and told Allen and Stuart, "I'm goin' in."

Allen regarded him warily. "You sure about this?"

"Yeah. Good to go. Let's do this thing and get out of here."

"What's the plan?"

"Gonna take it back to Bernstein and blow it in the UXO pit. Done it a hundred times."

Stuart asked, "UXO?"

"Unexploded ordnance." Boomer fastened the belt around his waist. "I'll be right back."

Boomer approached the artillery round on foot. His only protection was his Kevlar helmet and armor vest. His only tools were in the belt.

He was accompanied by a three-man security team from the escort platoon. Bomb disposal experts were high value targets for insurgent snipers.

Fifty yards out, Boomer called to his bodyguards, "You guys stay back! I'm goin' alone from here!"

Sweat dripped from the bomb tech's face as he knelt over the artillery round. In spite of its benign appearance, Boomer felt uneasy. He tried to calm his nerves. *Shake it off.* He thought of his wife and son back home. "Focus, dammit."

Stuart tried to duck behind a Humvee, but Allen snatched him up by the collar and snarled, "Can't do your job from down there, Doc."

Boomer inspected the artillery round again and still saw no triggers. As he carefully lifted it from the ground, his eye caught something protruding from the ground underneath the shell. A wire. Not a wire, an antenna.

Oh, God! It's a trap!

In a moment that seemed an eternity, Boomer set the round down and reached to his belt for the wire cutters. He had to cut the antenna. If he was quick enough, he could stop the remote signal from setting off the bomb.

Stuart and Allen watched Boomer pick up the round, then quickly set it down again. He then reached hastily for something from his tool belt. Something was wrong.

Stuart uttered, "What-"

Boomer disappeared in a sudden swirling cloud of dust, fire, and white hot shrapnel. The shock wave knocked his bodyguards to the ground. The next instant, Stuart heard the boom and felt the concussion. As the echo faded, he saw something fall to earth. It was a large, tattered object the blast had sent high into the air. As the mass thudded to the ground, Stuart realized it was the remnant of Boomer's torso.

17

Stuart returned to base hours later and slunk back to the quad. He flopped into his chair and dug the last flask of J.D. Black from his duffel. He grabbed the figurine from its bag and set it on the desk. He sloshed the flagon as he contemplated the artifact.

He put the booze away as his door sprang open. The unexpected light blinded Stuart.

"Hey, Doc!" It was Babauta. "You needing some air. Let's go."

"Do I have a choice?"

"Nope."

"Where are we going?"

"Hajji shop. Where else?"

Stuart walked into the sunlight. "Where's the Humvee?"

"We walking. Good for ya."

Hadi ran to meet them. On the way to the shop, they paused to watch the base's three M109 self-propelled howitzers conduct a fire mission. Each fired three high-explosive rounds in rapid succession.

The concussion of each shot pounded Stuart's chest. Hadi latched onto the professor's leg and covered his ears. Stuart's mouth went dry as images of Boomer replayed in his mind. He tried to block it out, but it was no use. He asked Babauta, "What are they shooting at?" He wanted to talk about anything but Boomer.

"Training mission. Dey doing it once in while for staying sharp."

"How do they decide where to shoot? They just pick a spot on the map and say, 'fire'?"

"No. Guns not shooting without *American* eyes on target. We not just picking a spot and shooting. We killing bunch of kids dat way."

"What if Iraqi soldiers ask for artillery?"

"Dat a *big* 'No, no'. I told you must having American observer before shooting."

"Don't you trust them?"

"If we shooting target on deir request and killing innocent people, still our fault."

At the hajji shop, they met Sergeant Parson and Specialist Vasquez. Parson gave Stuart a cola and said, "It's been rough mornin'."

"Yeah. I've had a few of those here."

"It's been rough for all of us. Boomer is the first."

"First what?"

"First KIA in the battalion."

"He told me he had a family."

"Yeah. He was goin' home in a few weeks for his son's birthday."

"Can we please talk about something else?"

"Sure, Doc." Parson looked at Hadi and asked, "Who's this?"

Stuart answered, "He followed us to the police station yesterday. He's staying here until we can find his family. When we found him in Tuz, he was carrying this." Stuart held up the statuette.

Vasquez crossed himself. "What is it?"

Parson said, "A demon."

"Well, we can't be sure." Stuart pointed to the inscription around the base, "The writing is primitive. I've never seen script quite like it. It may be a forerunner to cuneiform. Some of the characters are the same. If it's authentic, it's very old. I spent most of the night trying to translate it, but I got a migraine and had to stop."

Vasquez looked uneasy. "If it's not a demon, what *is* it?"

"I think it's some kind of idol. I've seen others like it, but the head is new to me. It might be some sort of god."

Stuart handed the object to Parson, but the veteran declined, "No thanks." He looked at Hadi. "Where'd he get it?"

"Don't know. I don't speak Kurdish, and he doesn't speak Arabic."

Parson said uneasily, "He needs to put it right back where he got it."

Ayad arrived with chai. "Perhaps I can help, Doctor? I speak both Arabic *and* Kurdish."

Stuart's eyes lit up. "Yes! Thank you. Please ask him where he got this."

Ayad conversed with the boy in Kurdish, then said, "He says he found it in a cave outside of Tuz."

This could be just what I'm looking for!

A rush of adrenaline shot through Stuart. "Ask him if there's more!"

Ayad conversed with the boy and said, "He will not say."

Stuart asked Ayad, "Have you ever seen anything like it?"

Ayad shook his head. "No. I am sorry my friend."

"That's okay. Thanks for your help."

Ayad smiled and put his hand over his heart. "It is my pleasure, my friends. I will check on your food."

Captain Crumm walked in and noticed the statue. "What the hell is that?"

Stuart answered excitedly, "It could be the greatest discovery in —"

Parson stepped in. "No big deal. Just some locals trafficking in stolen artifacts." He thrust the bag at Stuart who put the idol away.

"Artifacts, eh? Sounds boring as hell. Still, if you come across something valuable…" Crumm sat a nearby table. "Ed! Get me something to eat! I'm starving!"

Stuart asked Parson, "What was that about?"

Parson looked to the front of the shop. "Your souvenir is already causin' trouble. It's gettin' the wrong kind of attention."

Stuart turned to see Colonel Saffa staring at him. His usual entourage surrounded him.

There was something about the man that made Stuart's skin crawl. "Did he see it?"

Parson shrugged. "It don't matter. He'll know about it soon enough. Nothin' happens here without him knowing. The whole thing stinks."

"I'll keep that in mind. Speaking of things that stink. Where can I get my laundry done?"

"Ain't no laundry here. You gotta clean it yourself."

"How?"

"We take 'em into the shower with us in a five gallon bucket and some laundry detergent. You churn the bucket with your foot while you wash. I've got an extra bucket you can use."

"Thanks." He looked around. "Are this shop and your quarters really the only places to hang out?"

"Yup."

"It must get monotonous."

"Monotonous?" Vasquez said, "I'm going outta my damn mind! I'd give my left nut just to go for a drive and not have to worry about gettin' blown up. I'm sick of IEDs, body armor, and this fuckin' anchor around my neck!" He held up his M16. "Monotonous? Shit! We passed monotonous months ago."

Parson raised a hand to scold Velasquez, but then clapped the youth gently on the shoulder.

"Is everything alright my friends?" Ayad stood at the table.

Babauta answered, "Him alright, Ed. Just blowin' off steam."

Ayad spoke to the group, "I understand." He touched his heart with is hand to demonstrate his sincerity. "Your meals are free today."

Parson shook his head. "We can't do that."

"It is already done." He then leaned down by Stuart and said quietly, "Beware of Colonel Saffa. He is very interested in you and your little friend."

Crumm walked to their table and said to Sergeant Parson, "Tell Captain Allen I haven't forgotten about last night. Then tell him to mind his own business if he knows what's good for him."

The captain moved on to Saffa's table where he was greeted warmly. He spoke briefly with the Iraqi colonel, then rose and walked quickly out of the shop.

*****

Captain Allen stood in the command center. He asked the soldier at the duty log, "Look again. Are you sure Crumm's guys didn't report anything last night?"

The soldier turned the computer screen so he and Allen could both see it. "No, sir. They didn't say anything."

"That's the problem. They should have reported in, even if they didn't find anything. What time did they return to base?"

The soldier scrolled through the log entries. "It doesn't say, sir."

Allen's eyes narrowed. "That's because they never left."

The captain clumped to his office and sank into his chair. He unstrapped his fake leg and set it aside. His absent foot was aching. The phantom pain was back. He rolled up his pant leg and massaged his raw stump.

Why didn't the Warlock work? Allen had to find the answer. He already had a feeling where the truth would lead.

There would be serious charges. After what happened the last time he found problems with Crumm's record keeping, Allen knew he couldn't depend on Thorne.

He sighed. "The bad guys are supposed to be *outside* the wire."

He scribbled a list of things to check: maintenance reports, duty logs, inventories.

Allen's heart filled with dread at the thought of another soldier sharing Boomer's fate. It was just a matter of time. Somebody had to do something and he didn't see anybody else doing anything to stop it.

He had an idea. "One thing about a remote detonator...It doesn't care who it kills." He grabbed the secure line to division headquarters. Crumm wasn't the only one with friends in high places.

*****

Stuart, Babauta, and the others drank chai in the hajji shop as Captain Allen arrived.

Allen joined them. "I have big news. Some VIPs are coming through our area. The new Iraqi minister of defense's convoy is traveling from Kirkuk to Baquba tomorrow morning. It'll come through here just before dawn. We have to provide an escort."

Stuart noticed several sets of ears perk up at Allen's statement – including Saffa's.

Parson whispered, "Sir. What are you doin'? You know we can't talk about that stuff here."

Allen motioned for the rest to follow him outside.

Once they were out of earshot from the shop, Parson asked, "What are doin' sir? Half of Tuz'll know about that convoy an hour from now."

Allen grinned. "I'm counting on it."

"What?"

"We know we have a leak, right?"

"Right."

"We might as well feed him something that's useful to us instead of the enemy."

"The convoy."

"There *is* no convoy. But false intelligence can be valuable, too. We'll use it to beat the bushes and see what comes out."

"What's the plan after they bite at the bait?"

"It'll be Al-Khayal's turn to get a nasty surprise."

*****

Ismael stared out the window of his safe house. His trap for the American bomb disposal soldier was a success. He personally detonated the device. Since then, he'd relived the glorious moment hundreds of times.

He took a long draw from his cigarette and closed his eyes. Again, he felt the shock wave. He heard the thunderclap. He saw the flash of holy lightening. It was Allah's will…and it was intoxicating.

Ismael's cell phone interrupted his reverie. The number was a familiar one.

"Hello…Yes. I understand. The highway north of Tuz before dawn. It will be done, *Insha Allah*."

He returned the phone to his pocket.

The midday call to prayer echoed across the landscape. He knelt in obedience.

This is only the beginning.

*****

Shadows were long on Bernstein as Stuart sat on his bunk, studying the statuette when Parson entered and said, "C'mon. There's somethin' you need to see."

The two walked to the air field. Stuart saw troops lining the way from the medical bunker to the runway.

He stood silently next to Parson as Boomer's flag draped body made its way to a waiting Blackhawk helicopter. Each trooper snapped to attention and gave a solemn salute as the remains passed by.

Stuart put his hand on his heart. He didn't know what else to do. He flinched with each volley of the twenty-one gun salute.

Taps played. The echo of the lone bugle passed through him on its way into the twilight. The tune would never sound the same to him again.

An honor guard placed Boomer on the Blackhawk. They saluted and marched to the edge of the helipad.

The chopper lifted off and flew west into the setting sun.

As it disappeared on the horizon, Parson said to Stuart, "Boomer was our first death. He won't be the last."

18

Ismael checked his watch – three hours till sunrise. He stepped into the hole by the side of the highway and knelt to inspect the final device. He was exhausted.

The bomb maker rose, stretching his aching back. He looked to the three artillery rounds he'd already prepared. They sat in similar holes, dug one hundred meters apart. The one farthest from him was equipped with a remote detonator attached to a cell phone whose number only he had. All four were wired in sequence to explode simultaneously.

Ismael wasn't just going to exterminate the minister of defense. He was going to slaughter the entire convoy.

He called to his men, "Hurry! Bury those three while I finish this one!"

*****

High in the Iraqi night, a C130 specially equipped with electronic countermeasures prowled the sky. It was there by Captain Allen's request – a call to an old active duty buddy now working in division headquarters.

As the aircraft neared Tuz, a gloved hand flipped a switch. Multiband radio frequencies bathed the terrain beneath for miles in all directions.

*****

Ismael checked the connections on the last device. He tugged the wires gently. One came loose. *Damn.*

He crouched to fix the disjunction. Just before the wire made contact, the other three rounds erupted in a fusillade of molten steel.

*****

Parson and Babauta sat in the command center with Captain Allen.

Parson checked his watch. "The E-C130 should be over the target area by now."

A sound like distant thunder echoed into the bunker.

Allen smiled. "Gotcha."

*****

The blast knocked Ismael to the bottom of his hole. His face mashed against the artillery round as the wall of flame passed overhead.

He lay there, stunned, blind and deaf. His only sensations were the cool steel of the shell on his cheek and the sting of cordite in his nose.

The survivors of Ismael's cell pulled him from the hole and threw him in a car. They had to get to the safe house. One of his men lay next to him covered in blood and unconscious.

Ismael asked the driver, "Where are the other two?"

The driver had to shout for his shell-shocked superior to hear his response. "Dead! Blown to pieces!"

He handed his phone to one of his team. "Call Al-Khayal. Tell him what has happened."

Ismael began to pray – trying to tune out the ringing in his ears.

Yesterday belonged to him. Today went to the infidels.

Insha Allah.

*****

Colonel Saffa rushed into the command center and demanded, "I must see Colonel Thorne!"

Allen sent a trooper to wake the battalion commander, then asked, "What's so urgent, Colonel?"

"We caught insurgents planting an IED. They were going to kill the minister of defense."

"Is that so?" Allen's face betrayed nothing.

"Yes. They linked four artillery rounds together. Three went off accidentally. The fourth is intact."

"Were any of them wounded?"

"Two were killed. The rest escaped."

"I thought you said you caught them."

Saffa backpedaled, "We tried."

Thorne arrived in pajamas and flip-flops – his eyes red and droopy due to the early hour. He ushered Saffa into his office and shut the door, completely ignoring Captain Allen.

Parson said, "Sir, it was less than five minutes after the bomb went off when Saffa got here. His men ain't even made it to the scene yet. How the hell did he know what happened?"

Allen said to his men, "I think we found our leak." He went to his office and returned with a handful of papers. "I'm going to pay Crumm a visit."

Parson asked, "Kinda early for a house call ain't it, sir?"

"Early bird gets the worm."

"Be careful, sir. Don't lose your temper."

Allen said furtively, "Of course not."

*****

Captain Allen banged on the door of Captain Crumm's quarters.

"Go away!" Crumm was still in bed.

The door flew open. Allen limped to the bunk and grabbed Crumm by the shirt. "The platoon that found the IED had a Warlock. It should've saved Boomer's life, but it didn't."

Crumm remarked smugly, "So?"

"That Warlock belonged to your company!"

Crumm spat, "Get the hell out of my room!"

"A secondary device was buried underneath the artillery round. It was a trap. When Boomer picked up the round, a triggerman detonated the hidden bomb by remote control." Allen pulled Crumm out of bed by his pajamas and threw him to the floor. "He never had a chance!"

Crumm gasped, "That Warlock's been down for weeks."

"I checked the maintenance reports." Allen held up a handful of papers. "These are the all of them for the last month. All say the same thing – Warlock: fully mission capable!" He threw the papers in Crumm's face.

"Let me go!" Crumm tried to get up.

"I'm not done." Allen shoved him back down. "You didn't even send your men to check the GSR contact last night! Dereliction of duty.

Falsifying official records. Then there's all you're missing shit – weapons, night vision goggles. Where did it go? Hell, I've even caught wind of a narcotics ring in your company! I'm taking you down. I don't give a shit if you are the colonel's golden boy."

Crumm pulled a pistol and stuck it in Allen's chest. "Get out."

"Go ahead and shoot if you think you'll get away with it."

"You know I will." Crumm grinned. "Like you said, I'm the golden boy."

*****

Stuart rose before dawn and went for a walk to clear his head.

The morning still held on to the coolness of the night before as he sat on the berm to watch the sun rise. The orange ball was obscured by the ever-present haze on the horizon. It was one of the most beautiful things he had ever seen.

He was suddenly aware of the warmth of the sun on his skin, the coolness of the breeze on his face. He looked to the sky and noticed there wasn't a single cloud – just a deep, clear, infinite blue. He was thankful to be alive – thankful he was able to experience these sensations. He was also haunted by the knowledge that Boomer would never know them again.

Near a bunker, Stuart encountered a bird picking a pine needle from a camouflage net. The needles in these nets came from the States. They were caught up when the equipment was packed for shipment to Iraq. The little homemaker flew to a nearby tree and wove the foreign needle into its nest.

Stuart smiled. *At least somebody's getting some good out of this.*

He pondered the odds of this Tennessee pine needle ending up a part of an Iraqi bird's nest. Mind boggling.

He felt like that pine needle. Who could he have predicted the sequence of events that brought him to this time and place? Was it random chance or part of some grand design? He didn't know, but was surprised to find he hoped for the latter.

*****

A sedan bearing U.S. Government tags pulled into Sharon Baxter's driveway. Her stomach lurched as she saw it approach from the kitchen window. The vehicle came to a stop. Two uniformed officers got out and walked to the door, passing a banner bearing a blue star.

Sharon opened the door before they knocked.

"Is this the Baxter residence?"

Sharon's voice was quivering. "Yes."

"Are you Sharon Baxter?"

She covered face and nodded. Tears ran down her cheeks.

Her son, Tommy, was playing upstairs in his room. He glimpsed a uniform in his window.

"Daddy's home!" His eyes lit up.

This is just like Daddy. His father loved to surprise him – especially on his birthday.

Tommy ran down the stairs as fast as he could. "Daddy!"

Then he saw his mother. Something was wrong.

"Mrs. Baxter, we regret to inform you that your husband, Staff Sergeant Bradley Baxter, was killed in action…"

Sharon couldn't hear the man anymore. She couldn't hear anything. She couldn't see or feel. She was in dark nothingness.

Then she heard a sound – a chilling, mournful, soul rending sound. Sharon ached for the pitiful creature making it. She wondered what could cause such sorrow.

Then she realized the sound was coming from her. She was back in her body, crumpled into a sobbing heap on the floor.

As he lay in bed with his mother that night, Tommy couldn't stop crying. He thought about the last time he saw his father. It had been mere days before he left for Iraq. The last memory Tommy had of him was looking out the window of his family's minivan as the teary eyed soldier waved goodbye. Tommy had unbuckled his seatbelt and climbed to the back window to see his daddy for as long as he could before he passed out of sight.

Tommy prayed with all his might for God to bring his father back – to see his silhouette in his bedroom door – to let his daddy tuck him in just one more time.

He saw his father that night. In his dreams, Tommy hugged him tightly. He held on with all his strength, knowing he had to say goodbye when morning came.

*****

After his walk, Stuart thought a shower would help sooth his aching bones. Every inch of his him was sore thanks to the body armor and jostling Humvees.

The shower water was briny, but at least it was warm. His stiff muscles were thankful for the modicum of mercy. He worked his hair into a thick lather and took a deep, relaxing breath. Stuart leaned into the hot water and let it wash over his head.

The stall rocked violently. His respite was cut short by the now too familiar crack of a nearby explosion. The ground shook under his feet. The booming concussion felt as if it would flatten the flimsy plywood shower.

A torrent of rock and molten steel pelted everything around him.

Oh, God! He had to run. He had to find cover.

Shampoo stung Stuart's eyes as he coiled his body, preparing to burst from the shower stall with all his might.

He made his move. Stuart ran at a full sprint toward the nearest structure he could make out with his burning, soapy eyes. He could barely see where he was going.

A shower shoe flew off. The next step brought his bare foot down onto the jagged gravel. He lost his balance and tumbled, end over end, across the ground.

As he lay nude, scraped, and bruised, Stuart realized there were no alarms. No shouting. No one rushing to battle stations. It was over.

Shadows fell across him. They belonged to Babauta and Parson.

The islander threw Stuart a towel. "You meeting Rocket Man."

"Who?"

"Rocket man. He shooting dat rocket at us. He living in a village north of here."

"You know who he is?"

Parson answered, "We do. Even arrested him once."

"Then why in the hell is he still launching rockets at us?"

"Due process."

"Due process?"

"Bad guys here got the same rights as in America. We're not even allowed to interrogate prisoners. We gotta get specially trained people here for that. And the methods *they're* allowed to use are less coercive than those used in police stations across America. Hell, they ain't even allowed to interrogate anymore. Now they conduct 'interviews' – like they're applying for a damn' job."

"I thought captives were sent off to Guantanimo or Abu Grahb?"

"No. They get their day in court after we catch 'em. We grabbed Rocket Man tree months ago and sent him up the chain. He came back five weeks later. Released due to lack of evidence. We even had to give the prick a ride home."

Babauta grinned. "Not all bad. When we dropping him off, I giving him a big hug in middle of village and thanking him real loud for helping us. He so scared, he pissing his pants."

Stuart asked, "Was he guilty?"

Parson answered, "We found rocket parts and fuse timers at his house. There wasn't a single attack while he was gone. They started up again three days after he got back. You tell me."

Stuart admitted, "Good point."

The islander grumbled, "Fuckin' politicians."

Stuart asked, "Were the Iraqi courts afraid to prosecute him?"

Parson answered, "The Iraqis didn't let him go. We did. He fell under U.S. military legal jurisdiction cuz he was accused of acts against American soldiers. If he was charged with crimes against Iraqis, we would've turned him over to them. That's how it works." The veteran sighed. "Our own damn guys let him go."

Stuart stated awkwardly, "I didn't know."

Parson replied flatly, "Not many Americans do."

19

Ismael sat, once again, in his safe house. He pondered the reversal in his fortunes. A day ago, he celebrated killing the American bomb soldier. This day, it was he who licked his wounds.

Two of his men were dead. Another lost an arm. Only two remained beside him. It didn't matter. His work would continue.

He got to his feet and gathered his things. There was much to be done. Another operation was afoot.

The evening call to prayer sounded. He dropped onto aching knees and bowed his head.

Yes, his work would continue.

Insha Allah.

*****

Stuart spent the next two days in the quad pondering his discovery. His only breaks were for the bathroom and hot chow.

The characters at the idol's base mystified him. They held the key unlocking the dark figure's secret. He studied it till his head ached, but couldn't decipher the inscription. He invariably ended up entranced – gazing for hours into the relic's cold, black eyes.

He was on his way to breakfast when he ran into Sergeant Parson.

"Doc, have you seen Captain Allen."

"No. Not since the other day at the hajji shop."

"Me neither. Somethin's wrong."

"I'm sure he'll turn up. He couldn't have gone far."

"I've searched the whole base. I'm goin' to the office to look for clues. Gimme a hand?"

"Sure."

Stuart and Parson entered the intelligence office to find Captain Crumm going through Allen's desk.

"Can I help you, sir?"

"Get outta my way." Crumm tried to push past them, but Parson blocked the way.

"Sir! Have you seen Captain Allen?"

"No."

"You sure? Last time I saw him, he was goin' to your bunker?"

"Never showed. Now get out of my way!" The captain hurried out of the office.

Parson's eyes narrowed. "What the hell was he lookin' for?" He locked the door and reached into a nook behind a filing cabinet. "Captain Allen thinks his hiding place is a secret, but I know the man better than he knows himself."

He retrieved a stack of records.

Stuart asked, "What are those?"

"Inventories, hand receipts, requisitions. All from Crumm's company." He spotted something. "What's this?"

Mixed in with the papers was a map of the area around Tuz.

Parson asked, "Where did Hadi say he found that ugly little statue?"

"A cave north of Tuz. Why?"

"Sounds like Captain Allen thought little statues weren't the only things hiding there."

Allen had traced a line through the mountain pass north of town in red pen. The path was labeled 'Smuggling Route.' Next to the red line, he'd drawn a circle on a mountainside and labeled it *'Cave – Recon ASAP.'*

Stuart asked, "How did he know where the cave is?"

"Don't know."

"You think he's there?"

"Maybe."

"Surely he didn't go alone."

"If he did, he needs our help." Parson pointed to the map. "Hadi can guide us there. But nobody can know about it…especially Crumm. I don't trust that weasel. We gotta do this on our own. You up for it?"

"Count me in."

"Good. We'll need Babauta."

"And Vasquez," Stuart added.

"No. Vasquez stays."

"How can we go alone when we're not allowed to leave base with less than three Humvees?"

Parson said slyly, "Leave that to me."

*****

Stuart stood in his quarters a few hours later. Hadi sat at the end of his bunk, happily devouring a Hooah Bar. The professor raised a water bottle. Trembling hands made it difficult to drink. He looked to his duffel – longing for the last flask.

Parson, Vasquez, and Babauta entered.

Parson asked Stuart, "You ready?"

"Yeah."

"Babauta'll drive. Vasquez'll stay here and monitor the radio in case we need help."

Vasquez's face turned red. "That's bullshit, Sarge! I never get do anything. I didn't sign up just to watch a fuckin' radio!"

"You'll do as you're told and watch your mouth!"

"Allen's my captain too. I want to help and I'm the only person besides you guys that knows what's going on. You need me."

"Alright. You can drive, but I don't like it one bit." He added, "And you'll do as I say. You copy?"

"Yes, Sergeant."

They mounted a Humvee and rolled to the gate, where a guard stopped them. "Sarge, you know you gotta have at least three vehicles to leave the base."

Parson answered, "We're meeting up with the Iraqi police. They're late."

The guard smirked. "As usual."

"We'll just go down the road a piece. If we don't see 'em, we'll come right back."

"I don't know about that, Sarge."

"We'll be right back. Scout's honor."

The guard laughed. "Okay. Go ahead."

The Humvee traveled east toward the mountains. Soon, they were in the foothills. Hadi pointed the way.

The hills around them grew taller and taller. Babauta called out, "Radio going dead! Mountains must be blocking signal!"

They arrived at a small dead end valley with mountains rising sharply on three sides. Hadi pointed excitedly out the windshield.

Parson said, "Must be close. We'll dismount here. Stuart, Hadi, and I will travel the rest of the way on foot. Vasquez, keep the engine runnin'. Babauta, you pull security from the gunner's hatch."

Babauta nodded. "Yes, Sergeant."

Hadi, Stuart, and Parson entered the cul-de-sac.

Parson looked around. "See any caves?"

Stuart wiped the sweat from his forehead. "No. Nothing."

Hadi ran to a pile of rocks a short distance away and stood by them. He then walked a straight line in another direction as if counting his steps. The two Americans followed.

Of course! Stuart laughed.

"What's so funny?"

"Doesn't that rock pile look familiar? It's the same in the fields outside Tuz." He pointed at Hadi. "He hid the entrance so well that no one would be able to find it but him. The farmer's son used the same rock piles that mark his father's fields to mark the location of the cave. Brilliant!"

Hadi squatted next to a mound of rocks and dirt butted up against the valley wall and dug with his hands. Stuart and Parson joined in.

Within minutes, they uncovered a small fissure in the rocky soil.

Cool air flowed over them like a dying breath from the abyss.

Parson bristled, "There are more things in heaven and earth, Horatio, than are dreamt of in your philosophy."

Stuart smiled. "You know Shakespeare?"

"Just the parts I understand."

Stuart laughed. "Are you afraid of ghosts, Sergeant?"

"No. I'm talkin' about death. You ever felt it, Doc?"

"I've seen plenty of it lately."

"No. I'm talkin' about feelin' it."

"Feeling death?"

"Yeah. The grim reaper. Movin' around you."

"No. You?"

Parson nodded. "I felt it the first time when a bulldozer rolled onto my uncle. He was still alive when I got to him, but there was nothing I could do. I felt it just before he died. A presence that chilled my soul and made me sick to my stomach. My hair stood on end. Felt like I was bein' watched, but nothin' was there.

"It was the same in Desert Storm. Bodies everywhere. And the smell. My God, the smell. The angel of death was there. Always watchin'… Always waitin'." Parson shivered.

"I felt it again with Boomer and the car bomb in Tuz. But it was different then. I felt it *before* those things happened. I felt death coming."

"Why are you telling me this?"

"I've got the same feeling now."

Stuart's stomach knotted up.

The veteran shrugged. "But that's only if you believe in that sort of thing."

Stuart forced a smile. "Let's hope you're wrong."

Parson removed the flashlight from his vest and looked inside. "Looks like a cavern. Pretty big, too."

"Let's get in there." Stuart's hands trembled with excitement.

This could be exactly what I came here for.

Parson hesitated. "We came here to find Captain Allen. He obviously ain't in there."

Stuart thought quickly, "Maybe not…But whatever he was looking for is in there. We've come this far. He would want us to check it out."

"I'd don't like it, but you got a point."

The three made their way to the narrow tunnel. Stuart spotted illustrations on the walls. They were filled with bloody images and grotesque beasts similar to the idol.

The professor's voice echoed, "Fascinating."

Hadi hid his eyes and hugged Stuart's leg.

Parson stepped backwards. "This is far enough. There's somethin' here, Doc. Somethin' that's best left alone."

"Look at that!" Stuart spotted an inscription below the images. The script was the same as that on the base of Hadi's statue.

"What's it say?"

"Probably a curse on anybody that disturbs the place." Stuart smiled. "But that's only if you believe in that sort of thing."

Stuart followed the wall to an image of a black beast looming over two warriors and a child.

Parson shuddered. "Look familiar?"

"Yeah," Stuart said uneasily. "You're starting to give me the creeps."

They slowly crept on until they reached the chamber. It was empty except for a huge jet black statue of a winged bull in its center. The monstrous head was identical to the one on Hadi's idol. The creature seemed to breathe as if carved from living stone.

Parson whispered, "The devil, as a roaring lion, walketh about, seeking whom he may devour."

Stuart whispered back, "First Peter, chapter five, verse eight."

Parson was surprised. "You know the Bible?"

"Just the parts I understand." Stuart grinned. "My parents made me go to Sunday school until the sixth grade."

Cautiously, they searched the room.

"I can feel that thing starin' at me," Parson said as he kept one eye on the statue, expecting it to come to life at any moment.

"Look at this!" Stuart aimed his light at the walls. They were covered with more bizarre, distorted, macabre images.

Parson shook his head. "We don't belong here."

"We won't be long." Stuart scanned the room. "If big ugly is all alone here, where did Hadi get the idol?"

Stuart's flashlight found Hadi kneeling on the floor, bowing to the dark figure.

A voice echoed into the chamber. Both men jumped. It was Babauta. He sounded urgent.

"We're coming!" Parson led the way to the cavern. Babauta had his head in the entrance.

Parson called out, "What's up?"

"Calling for us on radio. Cap'n Allen saying we getting back to base right now."

"Allen's at the base?"

"Yeah. Sounding like someting big going down."

"On our way!" Parson called to Stuart and Hadi, "Let's go."

"No! We just got here," Stuart protested.

"Zip it, Doc! Let's go!"

Parson hurried Hadi and Stuart out before climbing through the narrow portal. "Did he say what it was?"

The islander shook his head. "No."

"I thought we lost radio contact."

Babauta answered, "We did. Not sure how, but da radio working again."

They traveled west toward Tuz until they reached the main highway and turned north.

*****

The Iraqi soldier kept a watchful eye from the window of his hiding place. The mud hut protected him from the sun's wrath. A bowl of grapes, a flask of water, binoculars, an AK74, and a Koran sat nearby.

He wiped the sweat from his forehead. The heat was oppressive in spite of the shade.

He'd been waiting here for hours. Traffic was light today. Only a few taxis and small cars had passed so far. He dreaded the thought of sitting there till dark, but he would if need be. Those were his orders.

As he finished the last of his grapes, he saw his target. An American Humvee drove toward him heading north.

The soldier raised the binoculars with one hand. With the other, he nervously gripped a remote detonator.

*****

Parson scanned the road for IEDs from the gunner's hatch as they sped back to Bernstein. Ahead, a dead dog lay to the right of the road – bloated by the hot sun.

Babauta swerved to the left shoulder.

When they were nearly abreast of the canine carcass, Parson saw it. An antenna protruded from the dog's distended belly. In a flash of understanding, he realized the animal wasn't bloated. It was stuffed with explosives.

The sergeant dropped through the gunner's hatch and yelled, "IED!"

The dog exploded in a searing conflagration of shrapnel and flame.

It was a nightmare made real. Time slowed as Stuart watched the fireball burst from the dog's corpse. A vision of hell filled Stuart's window as fire engulfed the Humvee. The vehicle rocked violently. Smoke filled the cabin. The noise was deafening.

Vasquez mashed the gas – trying to escape the kill zone.

"Is anybody hit?" Parson looked at the other passengers. "Doc! You and Hadi alright?"

Stuart checked the boy. "We're okay."

Vasquez stopped after a half mile, pulled the rosary from his shirt, and kissed it.

Parson and Babauta dismounted to inspect the damage. The Humvee's plate armor was deeply gouged, but intact.

Parson yelled, "Looks okay! Let's get the hell outta here!" They quickly mounted up and set off.

The window next to Stuart's head was cracked, but unpierced. It had done its job. During the remainder of the trip back to Bernstein, he didn't take his eyes off the smashed Plexiglas inches from his face.

20

Captain Allen stood before a group of officers and NCOs of the battalion. His face was drawn and cadaverous. Dark circles ringed his cold, sunken eyes.

The men were crowded into a shack covered by an old Iraqi aircraft hangar. The room was dimly lit by flickering florescent bulbs. The walls of the small space were covered in maps, charts, sketches, and photographs. The smell of diesel fuel and dust permeated the space.

A diagram depicting a section of Sulayman Bak was clipped to a dry erase board next to the captain. Several pictures of a house in this neighborhood were taped around the edges.

Allen pointed to the diagram. "I have intelligence indicating the bastard that killed Boomer is hiding out in Sulayman Bak. I'm gonna get the son of a bitch. And I'm going tonight."

He stepped to the entrance. "I asked you all here because you're the best leaders in this battalion. Before I go any further, you need to know something: This mission is *not* approved by Colonel Thorne. There could be severe consequences for anyone that takes part." He opened the door. "If anybody wants out, now's the time."

No one budged.

Allen locked the door and limped back to the front – looking each man in the eye. "Surprise will be our greatest weapon. Secrecy must be maintained. For this reason, you will not tell anyone about tonight's mission or our target. You will tell your men only what they need to know. They will be fully briefed once we reach our staging area just north of Sulayman Bak. You will tell your Iraqi translators absolutely nothing. They'll be ready to go at a moment's notice. That's their job."

Allen motioned someone forward. A black-clad Iraqi came forth from the rear of the room. The soldiers were stunned. No one had noticed the dark stranger.

"This is Fedallah. He's our source. He answers only to me."

The dark guest bowed his head and returned to the shadows.

The commander pointed to a lieutenant sitting in a lawn chair. "First platoon, you're the assault force. You'll go in the house and retrieve the target."

"Yes, sir."

He turned to another young officer standing at the side of the room. "Second platoon, you'll establish an inner cordon around the house. Nothing gets in or out. Got it?"

"Roger, sir!"

"Third Platoon, you're the outer perimeter. You'll also be the reserve."

"Good to go, sir."

Allen looked at his watch. "It is 1345 hours. Have your vehicles, equipment, and personnel in front of this hangar at 1600 hours for inspection. We'll depart for the staging area at 1700 hours. The operations order will be given to the entire group there. Any questions?"

Silence.

"Good. Map overlays of the route and objective for each of you are by the door."

He picked up a hammer and a piece of paper. "This is a signed and approved two-week leave."

He dug a nail from his pocket and pounded it through the paper and into the wall. "The name and dates are blank. It'll go to the trooper that captures – or kills – Al-Khayal."

Allen brought himself fully upright and rigid then roared, "Group! AttenTION!"

Every man in the room shot up from his chair and stood erect at the position of attention.

The captain barked, "Fall out!"

His men thundered their war cry in unison, "Raiders!"

*****

Ismael entered the safe house through the side door. He'd worked all night in a cramped Tuz garage preparing his next attack. The high tempo was wearing on him. He was exhausted, but proud to be doing the work of Allah.

He went to the bathroom to wash his hands. The water was hot to the touch. It came from an open-topped cistern filled with brown, salty water located atop the home.

He turned the water off and trudged into the small guest room.

As he lay sweating on the thin plastic pad, Ismael's mind still turned. Something dug into his hip. He reached into his pocket and pulled out a pair of wire cutters. With a grunt, he laid them aside and tried to get comfortable.

Ismael hadn't intended to work so late into the day, but he felt better knowing the car bomb was ready. All that remained was to finish the explosive vest. It would only take a few hours.

His eyelids became heavy. He drifted off to sleep. Soon, it would be the Arab collaborators' turn to feel the heat of his righteous, cleansing flames.

*****

Stuart, Parson, and the others found Allen with Fedallah in the hangar.

A chill went through Stuart. He recognized the shadowy Iraqi from the late-night sighting in P-quad.

Parson approached Allen. He was shocked by the captain's grisly appearance. "Sir! Where've you been?"

The captain ignored the question. "You, Babauta, and Vasquez cross rifles."

"Where've you been?"

"Doing what had to be done."

Parson pointed to Fedallah. "Who's this?"

"He's here to help us catch Al-Khayal."

"Did you really put up your leave as a reward for catching Al-Khayal?"

"Yes."

"Sir, you can't do that. You gotta go home to see your family."

"I can't see them until this is done. They don't exist until this is done."

Parson cut his eyes at Babauta. This wasn't the Captain Allen they knew.

Allen ordered, "Three of you, cross your rifles."

"Sir, what-"

"Just do it!"

Parson, Vasquez, and Babauta reluctantly complied.

Allen held out his hand. Fedallah pulled a knife, startling the group. The stranger drew the blade across the captain's palm.

Allen held his clenched fist over the crossed barrels. Blood trickled onto them.

Parson withdrew his weapon before the sanguine fluid touched it. "What the hell are you doin'?"

Fedallah said with a thick, raspy Arab accent, "The one you seek hides in shadows. To find him, we must have help from the shadows. They need something in return…a blood sacrifice."

Parson shook his head. "No. I won't do it."

Allen stared coldly at the sergeant. "It has to be done, Buck. More of our men will die if you don't." He pointed to Vasquez and Babauta. "What if Flask or Stubb is next?"

Vasquez was befuddled. "Who is Flask? What the hell is he talkin' about?"

Parson ordered Vasquez, "Get outta here."

The trooper looked confusedly from Parson to Allen.

The sergeant barked, "I said get go!"

Vasquez ran out of the hangar.

Parson returned to the group. His eyes bored into Captain Allen. "Damn you."

Fedallah gave the hint of a smile.

"The spirits require three." Allen called to Stuart, "Doctor Knight! You'll be the third. If you want to see something other than your quarters the rest of your time here, you'll join Buck and Stubb and give me your hand."

"Who the hell are Buck and Stubb?" Stuart looked to Babauta for help, but found none. He reluctantly clasped his hand on the crossed rifles.

Allen grasped the gathering tightly. Blood ran from the wound onto the barrels and Stuart's hand.

Fedallah produced a piece of parchment. He burned the vellum over the gathering as he recited an incantation in Arabic.

Parson tugged his rifle, but Allen's grip was iron.

When Fedallah finished, he said simply, "It is done. The djinn are satisfied."

Allen released his hold.

Parson glared at his captain. "You've damned us." His words were full of fury. "I'll go tonight to look after Vasquez," he said, "but I'm done with the rest of it. I'm done with you and your ghosts. You're on your own."

The sergeant stormed out of the hangar and into the darkness.

*****

Four hours later, Specialist Vasquez sat on the hood of a Humvee among the men of B Company's 1st platoon. The ad hoc company was assembled in a scrubby field a few miles north of Sulayman Bak. Captain Allen had given the operation order. Every man knew exactly what was expected of him.

Vasquez volunteered for the assault team. It was their job to break into the house and grab the target.

A private sat next to him with an M240 machine gun cradled in his lap. Vasquez said, "I can't believe we're gonna get the bastard that killed Boomer."

"We ain't got him yet, pup." Parson came out of nowhere. "The mission rehearsal starts in ten minutes. You two got plenty to be doin' besides sittin' there jawin'."

"Yes, Sergeant." Vasquez asked, "What was all that shit back at the base? And why did Captain Allen call me Flask?"

Parson spit a glob of tobacco juice to the ground. "Damn black magic. Just keep it to yourself for now. Stay focused…and stay away from Allen."

"Sarge, I thought you quit chewin'."

"I did." He turned and walked away.

"You okay, Sarge?"

The veteran faded back into the night.

21

Faisal closed his shop early. Other matters monopolized his thoughts. The brat had escaped again. Anger swelled in him like a pressure cooker about to explode. It was unacceptable.

Does he really believe the Americans can protect him?

But the boy wasn't his only concern. Faisal had been threatened like a criminal in his own business. He would have his revenge against the arrogant American captain and the traitor policeman as well.

A malevolent grin came to Faisal's lips. He knew exactly who could help him get his retribution.

As he sped home in his BMW, Faisal decided to pay Hadi's family a visit in the morning. His face would be the last thing they would ever see. The thought comforted him. His grin widened as the warm afternoon air blew across his face.

*****

The crimson sun hung low as Faisal entered through the front door of his Sulayman Bak home. He didn't bother to turn a light on. He just sat in his favorite chair and lit a cigarette – watching the smoke dance in the last rays of the day's light.

His cousin, the "holy warrior," was asleep in the small alcove of a guest room. At first, Faisal wasn't happy about the man staying in his house. But he now saw a way to use the situation to his advantage.

*****

The men were ready. The Humvees were loaded. The order was given. Rehearsals and inspections were complete. All questions were answered. Now it was just a matter of waiting for nightfall.

The radio in Allen's vehicle hissed and popped. "Raider 2, this is Charlie Lookout, over."

Allen picked up the hand mic. "This is Raider 2. Go ahead Charlie Lookout." Allen had placed a three-man observation team with high-powered optics hours ago. They were hidden in a position with a commanding view of the target house and surrounding area.

A short burst of static was followed by the team's report. "Roger. A second adult male has entered the target house. Couldn't tell if he was armed. No one else known to be inside at this time, over."

"Good copy, Charlie Lookout. Continue to observe and report. Raider 2 out." Allen switched handsets and disseminated this new intelligence to the rest of his team.

He looked west and saw the sun flirting with the horizon. It wouldn't be long now.

*****

An hour later, it was dark. Looking out the windshield, Vasquez counted nine Humvees staged in front of him. All engines were still. The entire company sat in silent darkness. The men sat – nerves on edge, muscles tensed – a hidden snake coiled and ready to strike.

The radio crackled. Allen's voice rang out in every vehicle. "All Raider elements, this is Raider 2. Short count in ten seconds." Ten seconds later, Allen keyed his handset again and began the short count. "5... 4... 3... 2... 1."

At that instant, every engine roared to life simultaneously. The 'short count' was used for decades by mechanized units to hide their numbers.

Allen broadcast again, "All elements report redcon status."

Each platoon leader reported back to Allen in sequence.

"Bravo 11, redcon 1."

"Charlie 21, redcon 1."

"Charlie 31, redcon 1."

They were ready. Allen gave the order. "All Raider elements. Execute move to target. I say again, all elements: Move-out time now."

The Humvees lurched forward, jostling across the nebulous Iraqi landscape en route to Sulayman Bak.

*****

Minutes later, the outer cordon was set. Vasquez's platoon parked their Humvees just outside it. They covered the rest of the way on foot to keep surprise on their side. They moved slowly and deliberately. Their night vision goggles scanned their surroundings as they progressed.

Another platoon walked slightly ahead. The squads of this platoon split off to form the inner cordon. All was going according to plan.

Allen, equipped with a radio on his back, limped a short distance behind the assault platoon. Stuart, Babauta, Fedallah, and an air support liaison were with him.

When the last of the lead platoon's squads had peeled off, a low voice transmitted from the handset of Allen's radio. "Raider, this is Charlie 21. Inner cordon set, over."

Allen keyed his hand mic. "Roger. Stand by." He turned to the air support liaison, "Sparkle the house as soon as I paint the door."

The sergeant nodded silently and whispered into his own radio.

Allen pulled flashlight-shaped object from his cargo pocket. He pointed it at the front door of the target house and turned it on.

To the naked eye, nothing happened. But those with night vision devices saw a wide beam of green light illuminate the home's entrance.

Then a massive beam of radiance, dwarfing Allen's light, shown down onto the house as if from heaven. Its source was a C130 cargo plane specially equipped with multiple cutting edge surveillance devices. It ensured that all participants in the raid knew exactly which house was the objective. It also enhanced the advantage provided by the soldiers' night vision goggles.

The house bathed in green light from above reminded Parson of the Nativity. *But we ain't bringing gifts and this guy ain't no babe in a manger.*

As his squad moved to their position at the front entrance, Vasquez whispered to the private charged with being the first one in the door. "Hey, let me go in first."

The soldier shook his head and whispered back, "No way, man. Parson'll kill me."

Vasquez sighed. "I'm tired of watching. Just once, I want to *do* something. I want to be a real part of this mission."

The private put up a finger. "Okay, but just this time."

Vasquez whispered, "Thanks. I owe you one."

*****

Faisal turned a light on, but there was no electricity. He took a drink from a bottle of bourbon on the small table by his chair. The room's only light was the orange glow of his cigarette.

Ismael rose from his slumber and entered the room. He spoke in a groggy voice, "Why don't you turn on a light?"

Faisal grunted, "The power is out."

Ismael smelled the alcohol as he groped for the chair next to Faisal's. "You must stop drinking, cousin. It is a sin. Allah will punish you if you do not repent."

Faisal took a gulp from his glass. "Then leave it between him and me." He took the last drag from his short cigarette. "I need a favor."

"What is it?" Ismael stiffened his neck, but it was too dark for Faisal to see him.

"A boy has stolen something from me. But he's under the protection of an American from the base. I need help eliminating the American and retrieving the boy."

Ismael scoffed. "Out of the question. I work to free our people. I'm not in the business of settling your personal vendettas."

"I have provided you with a safe haven at great personal risk. I have not asked anything in return until now. You *owe* me, cousin."

"Very well. There is a mission in a few days that requires my full attention. After that, I will see what I can do."

Faisal lit another cigarette. "Thank you, cousin. I am glad we could come to an agreement."

The cigarette lit his smiling face with an eerie glow.

Faisal congratulated himself. *I always win.*

The front door burst inward. Both men shot up from their seats.

Faisal saw a silhouette where his front door used to be. He grabbed the pistol from the small of his back and fired into the figure. It crumpled to the floor.

Faisal heard his cousin run for the side door. The next thing he heard was the report of three more shots. They came from the doorway where he shot the intruder. The rapid, blinding bursts of light left their impressions on his retinas like the strobe flash of a high-speed camera.

Pain shot deep into Faisal's hip, stomach, and chest. He fell backwards, knocking over the table that held his bourbon. He heard shouts, but they seemed to be getting further and further away. The afterimage of the flashes was fading. Faisal's entire body was numb. He was cold. He couldn't remember where he was. Then it all faded into nothingness.

Ismael jumped through the side door. He found himself surrounded by a squad of American soldiers with their weapons aimed at him.

He surrendered immediately.

"MEDIC! MEDIC!" A soldier shouted as he knelt over Vasquez's motionless form.

*****

A taxi approached the outer cordon. The driver had come to take Ismael back to his workshop in Tuz.

The soldier atop the nearest Humvee waved the taxi off with one hand, using the other to aim an M240 machine gun at it.

The driver didn't panic. He calmly turned his taxi around and drove back toward Tuz.

Al-Khayal will not be happy.

*****

Vasquez heard yelling and movement all around him, but saw nothing. Was he alive, dead, or somewhere in between? *If I can just move my arm, I'll know I'm alive.*

Burning pain jolted from his shoulder to his fingertips. He tried the limb. It wouldn't move. He tried the other arm. It worked. He raised a gloved hand to his face. He could feel the leather and Nomex fabric on his skin. He saw shapes as his eyes adjusted to the darkness. He realized someone was speaking to him. He looked up at the voice.

"Vasquez! Where are you hit?" Parson was doing his best in the dark to search him for wounds.

"My arm hurts like hell." Vasquez tried to sit up.

Parson felt the limb. It was hot. The young troopers sleeve was covered in blood. "Dammit!" The sergeant yelled to someone Vasquez couldn't see. "He's hit! Get the medic, dammit!"

Parson looked Vasquez over. "You hit anywhere else?"

Vasquez shook his head. "I don't think so." Parson helped him get slowly to his feet. The sergeant stayed by his side as they stumbled back down the street past Captain Allen.

A medic ran up to the pair and helped get Vasquez to the nearest Humvee where he used a flashlight to check for bullet wounds. "He's got one in the arm. I don't see anymore." The medic cut the sleeve from Vasquez's arm and examined the injury. "The round went through clean – missed the bone and blood vessels. It'll hurt like hell, but you'll be fine. Looks like your lucky day."

Vasquez gritted his teeth. "Yeah. Lucky me."

*****

Ismael was on his knees in the front room of Faisal's house. His hands were bound behind his back. Two soldiers stood over him. His cousin's body lay a few feet away. The flashlights attached to the Americans' armored vests flashed around the room.

Stuart and Babauta stood nearby. The doctor was surprise at how little it bothered him to be so close to the dead body. He felt as if he'd lost a part of himself without knowing it.

Allen was on the other side of the room in conference with the leader of his assault platoon. He said in a hushed voice, "What've you got?"

The lieutenant replied, "Sir, we've finished searching the house. We found a pair of wire cutters next to a sleeping pad in the small room by the bathroom. We also found a blasting cap in this guy's pocket." He motioned his head toward Ismael.

"Good work. That's all we need to nail his ass."

The platoon leader held out two Iraqi identification cards, one of them smeared with blood. "The detainee claims to be the dead guy's cousin visiting from Kirkuk. Both of them have the same third name, so it's probably true."

Stuart whispered to Babauta, "What's he talking about?"

140

"Dat how dey doing it here. Parents choosing boy's first name. Da second name his father's given name. Third name is grandfather's. It going on like this as far as he remembering."

"So the same second name means they have the same father and the same third name means they have the same grandfather."

"Right."

Allen glanced at his prisoner and asked Fedallah, "Al-Khayal?"

Fedallah shook his head.

Allen stood in front of Ismael, who stared at his cousin's corpse. The captain said, "You speak English?"

No answer.

"Where is Al-Khayal?"

Still no answer.

Allen yelled, "Doctor Knight! Get over here and translate!" The captain's eyes blared. "You're under arrest for the murder of Staff Sergeant Bradley Baxter." He drew back and smashed his fist into Ismael's face.

The prisoner hit the floor, then got back to his knees.

Stuart protested, "You can't do that! He's a prisoner of war!"

Allen kicked Ismael in the gut. "He's not a P.O.W., he's a saboteur. The Geneva Convention means jack shit to him."

Ismael lay in a ball on the floor. He coughed and rattled off a sharp reply in Arabic.

Stuart translated, "He says he's not a terrorist. He's here from Kirkuk to visit his poor cousin. He says we're the murderers and have broken into a peaceful home and killed an innocent man."

Allen turned his glance to the dead shopkeeper. "He shot one of my men. That was a stupid thing to do." He said to his captive, "You should worry about your own skin." He then told the platoon leader, "Get him out of here."

It was after midnight when the last American soldier returned to Bernstein. Everyone was exhausted, but the satisfaction of catching the man who killed one of their own was welcomed.

Ismael was taken to the base detention center where he was given a bed, a blanket, and a meal.

Colonel Thorne met Allen as soon as he dismounted his Humvee. A smiling Crumm stood behind him.

Thorne fumed, "My office. Now!"

22

Allen stood at attention in Thorne's office.

The colonel's face was bright red. "I should put you under arrest."

Allen didn't respond.

"You're damn lucky your little operation was successful. This was Captain Crumm's sector. It should have been *his* raid. Why did you go rogue with this?"

"Security concerns, sir."

Thorne shot him a poisonous look. "Are you saying Captain Crumm can't be trusted? Are you saying *I* can't be trusted?"

"Your words, sir. Not mine."

Thorne looked about to explode. "Enough! You're relieved! You're also restricted to base until I decide what to do with you. Colonel Saffa has requested we transfer your detainee to his side of the base. I've granted that request."

"Transfer? Are you insane? He killed Boomer! He killed one of *your* men! This guy falls under *our* jurisdiction!"

"If you recall, Captain, he also killed a bunch of Iraqis with a car bomb not long ago. Saffa has every right to take him to his side of the base. This prisoner will be tried in the Iraqi court system for crimes against the Iraqi people."

Allen protested, "He was captured by American troops. One of our men was shot capturing him."

"That was your fault. You sent the kid into this guy's house."

Allen bristled, but held his tongue.

Thorne looked satisfied with his words' effect. "This suspect is going to be turned over to the Iraqis. That's the end of it. I've made my decision. Transfer the detainee within the hour." Thorne picked a paper from his desk and pretended to study it. "You're dismissed."

Allen got in the colonel's face. "This is bullshit and you know it!" He stared his commander in the eye. "Sometimes I wonder which side you're really on."

Thorne spat, "Get the hell out of here!"
Allen marched out of the room, slamming the door behind him.

*****

Allen pounded his fist on the hood of his Humvee, then drove to the detention center. He bound Ismael's hands and feet before stuffing him into the vehicle.

The captain drove to an isolated part of the base near the perimeter. There was no light here. He dragged Ismael out of the vehicle and tossed him to the ground.

The insurgent rose to his knees. Allen stood in front of him. "Who is Al-Khayal?"

Silence.

"What's his name?"

Ismael merely stared ahead.

Allen pulled out his pistol. He charged the weapon and put it to Ismael's forehead. "Tell me or I'll blow your fuckin' head off."

Ismael began to chant softly, "Allah-u-akbar. Allah-u-akbar. Alaaaaaah-u-akbar."

"Shut up."

Ismael closed his eyes. His mantra grew louder.

"I said shut up!"

*****

Stuart sat alone in his quarters, still unable to crack the idol's hidden message. He considered enlisting the help of some of his colleagues in America, but then thought better. No one could be trusted. The history of archaeology was dotted with skullduggery and backstabbing. In the quest for fame and glory, the halls of academia could be as cutthroat as a back alley in Baghdad.

A sharp 'pop' sounded in the distance. He barely noticed it. He sighed. It hadn't taken him long to grow accustomed to the sounds of war.

*****

Ismael slumped to the ground, screaming. His ears were ringing. Cordite stung his nostrils. His leg was on fire. He opened his eyes. Blood gushed from his thigh. Looking up, he saw a smoking barrel.

Allen put the weapon to his prisoner's forehead and said coldly, "I know you speak English. Tell me who Al-Khayal is or the next one'll be higher."

Ismael renewed his chant with a trembling voice, "Allah-u-akbar. Allah-u-akbar. Alaaaaaah-u-akbar."

"Shut up!" Allen gripped the pistol tightly, his finger tense on the trigger. The bomb maker stared at the captain with contempt.

Allen caught a shadow in the corner of his eye. He raised his pistol. "Who's there?" Boomer's pale form stood next to the Humvee. His visage bore a look of disapproval. Allen said, "I have to do it. You know I do."

Darkness gnawed at the edges of Boomer's form until the specter faded into nothing.

The captain's pistol smashed into Ismael's head with a crack. The bomb maker collapsed, unconscious, into the sand.

"Fuck you. I'll find him myself." Allen tossed him into the back of the vehicle.

When Allen handed Ismael over to the Iraqis, a guard said with a smug smile, "Thank you for the help, Captain."

"Go to hell." Allen punched the gas and sped back to his side of the base.

*****

Later that night, Ismael sat in the Iraqi Army's detention center. In comparison, the American side was a five-star hotel. His new accommodations consisted of a wire mesh cage reeking of shit and rot. He had no food, water, or bed.

He lay curled in a corner of the pen, trying not to think about his leg, when a visitor appeared out of the darkness. The broad frame stopped in front of Ismael's cage and lit a cigarette. The glowing tip illuminated the visitor's face. It was Colonel Saffa.

Ismael was relieved. "Colonel, it is good to see you. Thank you for delivering me from the infidels."

Saffa smiled. "You are welcome, my friend. Are you comfortable?"

"Of course not. This cage is filthy. Please release me now."

The colonel ignored the plea. "Did your cousin mention anything unusual before he died? Anything about a boy or a small statue."

"Yes. Before the infidels broke into the house, he asked me to help him kill an American soldier. He protects a boy that stole something from him. He didn't say what it was."

"Thank you, my friend. This information will be most useful."

"When will I be released?"

Saffa shook his head. "It is not to be, my friend. I must keep the trust of the Americans. I cannot allow you to escape." The colonel flicked his cigarette to the ground. "On the other hand, you must not be put on trial, either."

Saffa's words washed over Ismael like icy water. "You don't mean…" He shook his head. "It cannot be."

Saffa nodded. "Yes. You understand. It is time to take your place among the martyrs. I envy the rewards you will receive in Paradise." He tossed a razor blade into the pen. "If you find you cannot carry out your final task before morning, you will be shot trying to escape." Saffa shrugged. "This would cause me…inconvenience. Your poor mother would suffer needlessly."

Ismael shook his cage violently. "You wouldn't dare!"

"I am sorry, my friend. My hands are tied." He turned and dissolved back into the darkness.

Ismael thought of the path that led him to this place. Grisly memories filled his head. The blood of countless innocents stained his hands. Was this really Allah's will? He thought of his family. Had he dedicated his life to the pursuit of justice, or squandered it in the name of revenge?

Doubt and regret found purchase in his mind. How many orphans had he made? How many grieving parents, husbands, wives? His savagery spawned hundreds, maybe thousands, more Ismaels – bitter, grief-stricken victims trying to bring meaning to the butchering of loved ones.

Was he any different from those that killed his family? Who was he to judge whose lives were forfeit?

He knew now that he'd been used. Al-Khayal used Ismael's anger to manipulate him just as Ismael had use religious zeal to dupe ignorant young men into becoming suicide bombers.

Ismael reached out with a trembling hand and picked up the razor blade. He tested its edge. It was sharp. That would make it easier.

Murderer or martyr? Ismael would find out soon.

Tears ran down his dirty face as Ismael slowly drew the razor across his throat.

Soft gurgling and deep sobs were the only sounds as the bomb maker's life oozed from him and mingled with his tears. After a last, ragged breath, all was still.

23

Allen stood in his office with Fedallah early the next day. "You promised me Al-Khayal! That was the deal!"

"I promised you the man that killed your friend. That is who you have."

"I had to turn him over to Saffa."

"That is not my fault, Captain."

Allen snarled, "No more games. Give me Al-Khayal."

Crumm appeared in the doorway. "I'll take it from here."

Allen scoffed, "Like hell you will."

"In case you forgot," Crumm smiled, "you've been relieved."

Allen stood nose to nose with his fellow captain. "You're startin' to piss me off."

"Back off, tough guy. You're already in enough trouble."

"What're you gonna do? Relieve me again?"

Crumm shook his head and chuckled. "He didn't tell you, did he?"

"Who?"

Crumm motioned to someone outside. "Get in here, Sergeant."

Parson shuffled shamefully into the room.

Allen asked his sergeant, "Do you want to tell me what the hell he's talking about?"

Parson stared at the floor.

Crumm sat in Allen's chair and put his feet on the desk. "The colonel's having you court martialed."

"On what charges?"

"Insubordination, refusing direct orders, conduct unbecoming…the list is as long as my arm. He's also declaring you mentally unfit. He had to after what Parson told him." He laughed again. "Did you really sprinkle blood on their rifles?"

Allen glowered at Parson.

The sergeant wouldn't look at him.

Crumm said lazily, "In a week, you're going to Speicher to be court marshaled. Until then, you're restricted to your quarters. Either you can

149

go on your own, or I'll be glad to arrange an escort. Parson will assume your duties for the time being."

Allen stared at Parson a long moment. The captain's face was a mixture of confusion, anger, and hurt. Parson still wouldn't meet his gaze. He stood in front of the sergeant and said, "Get outta my way, Judas." His former subordinate stepped aside.

The disgraced officer limped to the door and motioned for Fedallah to follow.

Crumm shook his head. "No. He's mine now."

Allen hobbled out of the building. The creak and clack of his fake leg on the floor echoed in the silent command center until the bunker's metal door shut behind him.

*****

Parson met Crumm in the intelligence office an hour later. He presented the captain with detailed maps of Yanijah, a town of about twenty thousand a few miles south of Bernstein. "Here's the map you wanted sir. They should be more useful than the ones you already got. I've also got some detailed aerial photographs of the neighborhood you'll be in. I'm working on more, but this is a good start, sir."

"Thanks. These'll come in handy."

"Fedallah should be able to give you more detailed information."

"Who?"

"Fedallah – the informant."

Crumm waved his hand dismissively. "Oh yeah, Allen's witchdoctor. I let him go."

"Let him go?"

"I had him removed from base. Good riddance. He gave me the creeps. We have what we need anyway." He grabbed the maps and turned to go. "We leave at sunset."

*****

It was late afternoon when Parson knocked on the door of Captain Crumm's living quarters. No answer. He knocked again, impatiently checking his watch.

A soldier came from a room down the hall and said, "Captain Crumm's doing his laundry out back."

Parson walked to the rear of the bunker and found Crumm hanging wet towels on a line. "What are you doin', sir? The mission starts in a few hours."

The commander waved him off. "It's under control. We have a pretty good idea what house the target's in. We just gotta go get him. It's not that complicated." He grabbed a dry towel from the line and said nonchalantly, "If you'll excuse me, I'm going to take a shower."

As Crumm walked away, Parson realized he'd made a deadly mistake.

*****

Word of the impending raid spread quickly across Bernstein. The battalion surgeon had assigned Vasquez to light duty, but he was determined to go. He had a buddy in Crumm's company – the driver for the first platoon leader. Vasquez called in a favor and got a ride in his Humvee. When he climbed into the back seat, he was surprised to see Stuart sitting on the opposite side.

They sat, sweating, in the belly of the armored beast until sundown. Stuart finally asked, "How's the arm?"

Vasquez held up the injured limb. It looked bigger than its counterpart due to the bandages under the sleeve. "Still hurts a lot, but the doc says it'll be fine in a few weeks."

"Good." Stuart checked his watch. "What's the holdup? I thought we were leaving at nightfall. That's what I heard at the hajji shop, anyway."

Vasquez yawned, "That's the plan. Must be running behind." He propped his chin on the butt of his M4 carbine. "I'm gonna take a nap."

Even with door propped open, the Humvee was crowded and stuffy. Stuart shifted in his seat and unfastened his body armor. "How can you sleep?"

"A soldier's gotta be able to go to sleep anytime, anywhere. First thing you learn in basic." He closed his eyes and relaxed.

A shadow fell across the young trooper just as he nodded off.

Vasquez looked up through squinted eyes as the intruder said, "You're in my seat." It was Sergeant Parson. "Get to the command bunker with Babauta."

"But Sarge-"
"Now."

*****

It was long past sunset. Crumm's company had waited in their Humvees for hours. Their captain sat in his bunker taking care of last minute details.

The lieutenant in the front of Parson's Humvee asked the veteran, "All I got is an aerial photograph of a neighborhood in Yanijah with one of the houses circled. We're already running late and haven't even got an operation order. You know anything else about this mission?"

"You know everything I know, sir. We'll just have to do the best we can with what we've got."

The young officer leader shook his head. "This is bullshit."

Parson gave Stuart a foreboding look. "You feel it."

Stuart nodded. He knew it wasn't a question.

Parson looked out the window into the gloom. "Death never leaves empty handed."

Ten minutes later, the commander finally appeared. As he mounted his Humvee, Crumm circled his hand above his head then pointed forward with a dramatic flourish. One by one, engines came to life. The company rolled out the south gate toward Yanijah.

*****

It was 2000 hours when Crumm and his company halted in plain view of the target house. Stuart could see eyes peeking at the Americans from darkened windows.

So much for the element of surprise.

Crumm looked at his aerial photos, trying to decide which house was the target. A reconnaissance would have helped, but it was too late for that. He pointed to a cluster of houses, "It must be one of those three. We'll just check 'em one at a time. Let's go!" Crumm gave the charge signal again and pointed at the first home.

The soldiers dismounted, but none moved to the house. No one knew who was supposed to be assaulting, over-watching, or cordoning the area. It was chaos.

The platoon leader said to Parson through gritted teeth, "We look like the fuckin' Keystone Cops."

"Couldn't have said it better myself, sir."

Crumm yelled in frustration, "I said move, idiots!" He grabbed the squad closest to him and sent them to the first house followed by the second. Both were empty except for some frightened Iraqi civilians.

Parson found a soldier talking to some residents through an Iraqi translator and asked, "What're they sayin'?"

"First he said he lives here. Now he says he's visiting from out of town. He said the bad guys were here but left. Then he changed his story and said he doesn't know anything. Just more bullshit circle talk."

Stuart asked Parson, "What's circle talk?"

The veteran answered, "Iraqis talk in circles – contradictin' themselves to avoid answering questions. It's frustratin' as hell."

When they entered the third house, the troops knew they had the right one. The residence was completely devoid of human life. There was no sign of insurgent activity except for one thing: a tortured, mutilated body. What was left of the poor wretch sat bound to a chair. It was Fedallah. A sign, handwritten in Arabic, hung around his neck.

Stuart looked upon the revolting display with jaded numbness. For once, he didn't have the urge to vomit.

A soldier asked, "What's the sign say?"

Stuart answered gravely, "It says traitor."

The trooper asked Crumm, "What do you wanna do with the body, sir."

"It's not our problem. Leave it." Crumm returned to his vehicle. "The house is empty. Mount up and head back to base!"

Parson approached Crumm as they walked back to their vehicles. "Sir, the bad guys knew we were comin'. We should take a different route back to base. I recommend circlin' to the east and enterin' through the north gate."

Crumm scoffed, "That would take at least forty minutes longer. Get in your vehicle and take the lead. Tell the L.T. to use the same route we took here."

"Sir, the enemy will be expec-"

"The same route, Sergeant!"

Parson saluted grimly headed back to his vehicle. He found Stuart and pointed into the darkness. "Our Humvee's over there. Just walk straight. Can't miss it."

"Aren't you coming?"

"I'm right behind ya. Remember those papers we found in the office?"

"Yes."

"Make sure Vasquez gets 'em. He'll know what to do."

"Why don't you give them to him?"

"Just get 'em to him. Now go on. I'll be along shortly."

Stuart wandered into the darkness. When he was out of sight, Parson set off in the opposite direction.

*****

Stuart spotted a Humvee. He opened the door and found it wasn't his. "Sorry! These things all look the same in the dark."

The driver waved him in. "C'mon in, Doc! We got room. I'll call the L.T. and tell him you're ridin' back with us."

"Thanks. It's really dark out there." Stuart climbed in as the company pulled out in single file.

*****

Allen sneaked into the command center to listen in on the radio traffic. Babauta and Vasquez were already there. They updated the captain on the mission's progress.

Allen was furious. "Crumm let Al-Khayal get away. That dumbass could fuck up a wet drea-"

"Raider X-Ray, this is Alpha-One. Returning to base on Route Valiant, time now, over." It was a radio message from Crumm's first platoon.

"Are they taking the same route back to the base?" Allen ordered Vasquez, "Tell Crumm he's got to take another route."

Crumm replied, "That'll take too long. We're going the short way."

Allen grabbed the hand mic, "Alpha 6, you've got to take another route. It's too dangerous to retrace your steps. Don't pattern yourself."

*****

Crumm turned off his radio and said to his driver, "I hate that guy."

*****

"Alpha 6! Alpha 6!" It was no use. Crumm wasn't answering.

Allen yelled to Babauta, "Get the Raven up! We can use it to scout the route ahead of 'em."

Vasquez pulled Parson's flash drive from his pocket and handed it to the soldier typing the duty log. "Copy the file onto this. If the shit hits the fan, we'll want a copy of what *really* happened."

*****

It was pitch-dark. The lieutenant was nervous. He wanted to get off of this road as soon as possible. He couldn't use misdirection to thwart the enemy, but speed was still an ally.

The driver suddenly stood on the brake. The vehicle ground to a halt. Someone had stretched concertina wire across the road, blocking their way.

The young officer's mind raced. He had to do something. "This is bad. This is very bad."

*****

The Raven circled two hundred feet above the convoy. Allen and the command center staff watched the real-time feed on the wall-mounted flat screen.

Babauta spotted something. "Contact! Tree hajjis at ten o'clock!"

Allen saw it immediately. "Shit! They've got an RPG!" He grabbed the hand mic again, "Any Alpha element! Contact at your ten o'clock! Three tangos with an RPG! Get out of there! I say again! Get out of there!"

A bright streak left the RPG and headed for the lead Humvee. Allen whispered, "Oh God."

*****

Parson saw a bright flash to his left, then watched the fireball approach like an expected visitor.

*****

A voice rang out over the command net, "All Alpha elements, this is Alpha 11. We have encountered an obstacle and are attempting to find a bypass at this ti- RPG! RPG! Get ou —"

The voice was cut short by the fiery shriek of a rocket-propelled grenade. The net went silent – except for the eerie static that echoed in the command center.

Allen watched it on the Raven's thermal video feed. The projectile penetrated into the crew compartment before exploding. Everyone on board was consumed in the conflagration. The Humvee burned brightly against the black desert floor.

*****

Radio traffic erupted into pandemonium as the attackers melted into the countryside.

Crumm crossed his arms and rocked in his seat. His driver said, "Sir! You gotta do something!"

Crumm yelled, "Go back to base!"

"What about our guys?"

"I said go back to base!"

The driver held out the hand mic. "You gotta give the order."

Crumm shouted, "You do it!"

*****

Crumm's Humvee pulled into the Alpha Company area on Bernstein minutes later. Parson's Humvee sat, burning where it had been hit, with the crew still inside.

Crumm turned to his driver with a sigh. "Tough night."

The driver didn't respond.

The Humvee stopped. Crumm opened his door and found Allen standing before him with clinched fists. He stepped from the vehicle and said with a scowl, "What's your fuckin' problem?"

Without a word, Allen crashed a fist into Crumm's jaw. Crumm collapsed like a rag doll.

Allen growled, "Get up."

Crumm curled into a fetal position.

Allen kicked him. "I said get up, you pussy!"

Crumm didn't budge.

"Have it your way." Allen straddled Crumm and pounded his face savagely. His anger swelled with each blow. Crumm screamed for his men to help, but none intervened. They just watched silently.

Allen howled with hate as he gave himself to his rage. His eyes burned with wrath. He was out of control.

Panting with fury, Allen drew back his arm, gathering his strength for the coup de grace.

As Allen's fist sped toward Crumm's face, something knocked him from his enemy's battered form.

It was Sergeant Babauta. "Cap'n Allen! Snap out of it!" He pulled Allen to his feet. "You getting outta here now, sir." He pulled Allen to his feet.

Allen turned and drew back to strike the sergeant, but lowered his fist as recognition broke through his frenzy. He looked blankly at Crumm's crumpled form. Without a word, the captain limped into the moonless night.

One by one, Crumm's troopers left too, leaving their commander whimpering in the sand.

*****

Stuart stumbled to the quad and fell onto his bunk. Parson was right. Death didn't leave empty handed.

I should've been in that Humvee. Parson saved my life.

How did he know what was going to happen?

He grabbed his duffel and pulled out his last bottle of Jack. He opened it and put the vessel to his lips. He paused. It didn't feel right in his hands anymore. He set it on his desk and stared at it for a long while.

Finally, he grabbed the whisky with a trembling hand. Stuart threw open the door and stepped into the night. He bellowed a primal yell into the darkness and hurled the bourbon against a concrete barrier. The bottle shattered. Its contents ran down the wall like pungent blood.

Stuart didn't know what he felt as he watched the liquid trickle to the ground. He only knew it was better than feeling nothing at all.

He fell onto his bunk. As Stuart lay there, a strange feeling came over him. Something was missing and it wasn't the alcohol. He sat up and scanned the room. Suddenly he knew what was absent. Panicked, he reached into the bag for the idol. It was gone.

24

The battalion had lost five men in a heartbeat. By the next morning, their remains were recovered and put under armed sentry in the medical bunker. The guard was changed every ten minutes to allow each volunteer the opportunity to stand watch. Blackhawk Helicopters were coming from Balad that afternoon to begin the fallen soldiers' journey home.

Stuart had spent the night tearing his quarters apart in search of the lost idol, only to find that his copy of *The Archaeology of Ancient Mesopotamia* was also missing.

Stuart had hardly slept in days. His dreams were increasingly terrifying. Every time he closed his eyes, he saw images of death. His friends. His family. All of them dead. Sometimes they looked like they were sleeping. Other times they were dismembered – blown apart. But they were always dead. The stench. The pallor of death on their skin. The milky stillness of their eyes.

The eyes. They were the worst part. They always stared at him… blaming him.

Stuart went for a walk. He didn't know what else to do.

Something unusual caught his fatigued eye as he surveyed the Bernstein skyline. Some rebellious soldiers flew the American flag at half-mast from an improvised flagpole in defiance of DOD policy. That was one thing that was actually in the brochure. America was in Iraq to liberate, not conquer. Consequently, troops were forbidden from displaying the very banner they were sworn to defend.

Originally, Stuart agreed with the policy, but now it just seemed stupid.

This wasn't an adventure anymore. As Stuart watched the flag flutter in the burning breeze, his reason for coming to Iraq now seemed trivial and selfish. Even the loss of the idol surrendered its sting.

He thought of the soldiers he'd met here. He felt a bond with these men. He'd shared their fear, their frustration, and their dangers.

He'd grown to respect them. Stuart knew he'd never be one of them, but at least he understood them.

I've wasted so much time. He let ambition and obsession with his work destroy his marriage. *And for what?* Stuart promised himself that, if he made it back home, he would live for the things that were truly important.

Near the command bunker, he saw a trench marked off with yellow caution tape.

The furrow had been dug to bury the power lines from a nearby generator to keep vehicles from running over them. While digging, the engineers uncovered an old ammunition cache. Machine gun rounds, hand grenades, and other ordnance jutted from the trench's walls.

Stuart thought of the history of this land – millennia of endless war.

He wondered if the sacrifices of the soldiers on Bernstein would end up like this cache – just one more layer of junk in the sand that no one remembered or cared about.

*****

Crumm sat with his supply sergeant, reviewing an inventory of the items lost in the destroyed Humvee.

The sergeant went over the list one last time, trying not to stare at Crumm's swollen face. "Well, sir. That's all of it. I'll submit these items as combat losses so the army don't come asking for 'em when we get home. We're gonna to have to answer for enough lost stuff as it is."

"Yeah. Captain Allen reminded me of it often."

"It is a lot of stuff, sir: machine guns, night vision devices, rifles. Somebody's gonna have to answer for it."

"Who's to say all those items weren't on that Humvee when it was destroyed?"

"Sir, you know damn well they weren't."

"Did you inspect that vehicle before it left the gate on last night's mission?"

"No sir, but-"

"Then you can't say for sure that the missing items weren't on that vehicle can you? Add 'em all to the list of items lost in last night's incident." Crumm leaned in. "Otherwise, one of us will go down hard… and it ain't gonna be me."

The sergeant stared coldly at Crumm. "What you're talking about is illegal. You won't get away with it."

"I know what you're thinking, Sergeant. Forget it. If you report this, it'll be your word against mine. I'm the best bull shitter of 'em all. I can feed you a bowl of dog shit and make you think it's ice cream. And don't forget which of us is the golden boy."

Crumm rose to leave. "I'll get out of here. You've got a lot of work to do." He paused. "You know those nice Nomex gloves you just got in? You have a few extra pairs now, put me down for one – make that two extra sets." Crumm winked. "A man can never have too many gloves."

*****

Stuart went for a walk at dusk and ran into Allen near the hajji shop. He was sitting in a lawn chair watching the sunset. The captain was unshaven, but looked better – less ashen than the last time he saw him. He had aspect of a weary man that had just cast off a heavy burden.

Stuart found himself a chair and sat next to him in silence. After the sun disappeared, Stuart said, "You look like shit!"

"Thanks."

"I thought Colonel Thorne restricted you to quarters."

"To hell with Thorne."

"How much trouble are you in?"

"Plenty. Thorne was furious about me decking Crumm. He seemed more upset about that than our guys getting killed. He bumped up the schedule. Choppers are coming for me tomorrow."

"I'm sorry."

"Don't sweat it. I got enough dirt on him and Crumm to bury 'em both if they want to push it."

Stuart unfastened Babauta's knife from his armored vest and gave it to Allen. "For good luck."

"What's this?" The captain said, surprised.

"Babauta gave it to me for protection, but you should have it. You need it more than I do."

Allen declined. "Keep it. They'll just take it from me when I'm detained for court martial."

"Humor me," Stuart insisted, "I'll feel better if you take it. Don't ask me why."

Allen took the knife. "Thanks." He smiled. "So what's on your agenda the next few days?"

"I'm helping with a medical clinic in Tuz tomorrow. They need a translator."

"Good. You'll enjoy that. It's the good part of what we do here."

Ayad appeared from inside the shop. "Hello, my friends." He said consolingly to Allen, "I heard about your soldiers. I am very sorry. They were good men."

"Yes, they were."

"I have also heard about what happened to you, Captain. Are you alright?"

"I'm fine."

Ayad gave Allen a sympathetic look. "We are closed, but I can make some food for you if you like. How about a nice kabob?"

"Not hungry. Thanks anyway."

"As you wish, my friend."

After Ayad left, Stuart asked Allen, "What's the deal between you and Crumm?"

"He's National Guard and I'm active duty."

"That's what Boomer told me. He also said you had a run in with him about some missing equipment. But I still don't get the hate. You're both supposed to be on the same team."

Allen said, "I tell you, as officers, that you will not eat, sleep, smoke, sit down or lie down until your soldiers have had a chance to do these things. If you do this, they will follow you to the ends of the earth. If you do not, I will break you in front of your regiments."

"I don't follow."

"My old battalion commander's favorite quote. It's from the speech a British general gave to his junior officers during World War Two. It sums up the active duty approach to being an officer. Lead by example. The troops come first. National Guard officers like Crumm and Thorne don't get it.

"The Guard's a part-time gig. The higher rank you are, the more time it takes from your real job. If you have a successful career out-side the Guard, sooner or later you reach a point where you gotta give up one or the other. Ultimately, the best and brightest get out. Others get promoted because they're drinking buddies with somebody in head-quarters. Then we go to war and men die because of them. Active duty promotes on merit. The National Guard promotes by attrition. That's how you get corrupt incompetents like Crumm and Thorne running the show. They are everything that's wrong with the Army."

"I see."

Ayad brought them tea. "At least have some chai, my friends."

Allen took the tea. "Thanks." After Ayad returned to the shop, he sighed. "Fuck it. Fuck Crumm. Fuck Thorne. Fuck this place. Fuck Al-Khayal. They can have it." He sighed, "Just gotta let it go. Boomer tried to tell me, but I wouldn't listen. You'd do well to take his advice, too."

Stuart chuckled. "I'm not chasing terrorists."

"Everybody's chasing something – you included. I think you know what I'm talking about." Allen watched Stuart squirm in his seat. "I know what you must think of me, but we're more alike than you think. We all have our ghosts." He stood. "Let yours go before it's too late." He walked off, leaving Stuart alone in the darkening gloom.

25

Stuart took Hadi to Ayad's shop the next morning. Ayad came to their table. "Hello, my friends! What can I get for you today?"

Stuart patted Hadi's shoulder. "Just grabbing a bite before I head out."

"Where are you going?"

"Tuz. I'll be gone for a while, so I wanted to make sure Hadi got something to eat before I left."

"He is not going with you?"

"No. Not this time." Stuart had an idea. "Would you mind keeping an eye on him while I'm gone?"

Ayad smiled. "I will take good care of him."

*****

Colonel Saffa watched Stuart and Hadi eat from across the shop. After Stuart left, he stood outside and watched the boy play in a clearing nearby.

Saffa needed to learn about the idol. It was certainly more than it than appeared. Judging by the American professor's reaction, it was valuable. He knew the boy found it in the mountains near Tuz, but that was all. A lack of knowledge meant a lack of control. This was unacceptable, for control was power. Saffa was master of all things under his gaze – especially valuable things.

Yes. He would know the idol's secrets. He would start with the boy. He would tell Saffa the location of the cave. The boy would tell him everything...one way or another.

Saffa approached the boy, but halted when a massive American sergeant stopped to play with the youngster. He decided to wait until the brat was without his protectors to make his move.

*****

Stuart rode to Tuz with the medical platoon. He was their translator for a one-day clinic. He hoped his weak Arabic would be sufficient. He looked up at Vasquez in the gunner's hatch. *Poor kid.* Vasquez blamed himself for Parson's death. He'd barely spoken since. Stuart was just thankful to have a familiar face along.

Stuart asked the medic next to him, "So, where's this clinic?"

"At a local school. There is no clinic until we get there."

"Why us?"

"It's the right thing to do. I don't see any bad guys helping these kids."

"How will people know about it?"

The medic grinned. "A row of Humvees parked in front of the school is better than a billboard."

When the convoy reached Tuz, Stuart watched the traffic, people, and buildings pass by his window. "Are we near the school?"

"We're makin' a stop at a gas station first."

"Why are we going to a gas station? We fueled up at the base."

"The clinic's not our only mission today. There are only two gas stations in Tuz. Last month, a fuel shortage caused lines a mile long at both of 'em. Caused a lot of problems. We're here to make sure this one's getting its supply."

"The whole country is one big oil field! How can there be gas shortage?"

"Iraq has no refineries. It's pumping oil out of the ground twenty-four hours a day, but it has to be sent to other countries for refinement, and then bought back."

Stuart sighed. "Nothing here is ever easy."

"Nope. It's not."

The platoon pulled into the gas station. The medic dismounted and stepped under an awning. Stuart joined him. Some sergeants walked to the pumps.

Stuart asked, "How much is gas here?"

"About fifteen cents a gallon. Black market dealers sell it for half that. They get their supply from corrupt officials in the oil ministry. When we catch the black marketers selling it, we just chase 'em off. We're not gonna shoot anybody over a few stupid gallons of gas."

"What do you do with the stuff you confiscate?"

"We give the next few cars that pass by free fill-ups."

This area of town was bustling with pedestrian traffic. Stuart guessed the neighborhood was Shiite since most of the women wore black burkas covering everything but their hands. He snapped a picture of one of these women walking with her two children.

A group of teenage boys with slicked back hair and spit curls approached. Stuart thought they looked like something from *Westside Story*. Two of them asked Stuart if he wanted some whiskey. One opened up his denim jacket to reveal a bottle of bourbon. Stuart politely declined.

No booze in Muslim countries…fucking State Department morons.

Stuart asked the medic, "Isn't this clinic risky? We're gonna be in one place a long time. We'll make a great target."

"Yeah. It's dangerous, but we gotta build trust with the people. You can't do that from inside a Humvee."

Children in a passing car waved. Stuart waved back.

Stuart felt a little hand take hold of his. He looked down and saw a child smiling up at him with big brown eyes. Stuart thought of Rachel. His heart melted. It had been so long since he'd held his own little girl's hand. Everything was different now. A different world. A different life. A different man.

*****

Lieutenant Hussein knelt in a mosque on the north side of town. It was Friday, the Muslim holy day. The place was filled with the faithful.

He heard shuffling behind him. It sounded like a man pacing while arguing hushedly with himself. Hussein didn't look back. He didn't want to embarrass the troubled worshiper.

Then the sound changed. It grew louder. The man began repeating the same phrase over and over.

"Allah-u-Akbar!" The chanting turned to shouting.

As Hussein rose to confront the noisemaker, he saw the explosive vest. It was connected to a thumb switch in the man's right hand.

"Allaaaaaaaaaaaah-u-Akbar!" The man held out his arms, closed his eyes and pressed the switch. Nothing happened. His eyes boggled in disbelief. He hit it again. Still nothing. The frustrated would-be bomber mashed the switch repeatedly without result. The vest was unfinished. Ismael died before he could complete it.

Hussein lunged at the intruder. The two men wrestled among the prayer mats. A well-placed knee to the groin freed the insurgent from Hussein's grasp.

The terrorist ran out of the Mosque and onto the street. Hussein followed him. The pair turned south and sprinted down the sidewalk. People came pouring from the Mosque doors behind them and scattered into the garbage strewn street.

Another bomber sat parked in a sedan near the entrance, shocked to see the policeman chasing his partner out of the shrine.

The plan was coming apart. His partner was supposed to set off the vest inside the mosque. Then he would set off his car bomb, killing the survivors and onlookers gathered outside. But everyone was running away. The place was nearly abandoned.

He decided to run for it. He was at peace with being a martyr, but he wasn't about to throw his life away in a botched attack.

He opened the car door. The dome light came on, completing the detonation circuit. The car erupted into fireball of contorted steel.

The explosion knocked Hussein and his quarry to the ground. Hussein was the first to rise. He dove and landed on top of the insurgent.

Hussein pinned the terrorist's arm behind his back and waited for help. He knew it would arrive soon. Car bombs drew a lot attention.

*****

Soon after the medical platoon arrived at the school, parents lined up with their children outside the run-down building.

Stuart helped unload supplies. He said to a medic, "Great turnout. I would've expected the locals to be more hesitant to get treatment from Americans."

The medic grabbed some medical supplies from his Humvee. "It's a good indicator of the neighborhood's attitude. These parents have to trust us to bring their kids here." He walked into the school's main lobby where the clinic was getting up and running. "Healthcare here sucks. Our field medics can give better treatment than the doctors at the local hospital." He grabbed a pair of latex gloves. "Let's get started!"

Stuart helped treat children for maladies ranging from burns to ear infections. Fortunately, his translating skills proved adequate. The verbal exchanges were short and simple.

Stuart helped treat a beautiful little girl the same age as his daughter. She had stepped on a broken bottle and badly cut her foot.

Stuart was helping the medic bandage the girl's wound when the platoon leader's voice echoed through the lobby, "Pack it up! We're rollin' out in five minutes! We've got a situation!"

*****

Hadi finally went back to the quad. Saffa looked around carefully. The boy's guardians were gone. This was the time. If he was going to grab the child, he had to do it now.

*****

The medics quickly shut down the clinic as their platoon leader updated them. "There's been another car bombing at a mosque in the northern part of town."

Stuart asked the lieutenant. "Are we going there to help with the casualties?"

The officer nodded. "Yes, sir. Details are still fuzzy. Captain Crumm should get there ahead of us. He was at the mayor's office when it went off." He called to his men, "C'mon! Let's get outta here!"

*****

Sergeant Babauta had grown fond of Hadi since the boy's arrival on Bernstein. He had brought some Hooah bars from the mess hall for him. *He liking dese.* Babauta smiled. He walked to the quad and knocked on Hadi's door. There was no answer, but he heard movement inside.

"Hadi? It's Sergeant Babauta. I having you some candy!"

*****

169

Saffa covered Hadi's mouth and pinned him to the ground. He pulled a knife. If the visitor didn't go away, he would have to dispatch him quietly.

*****

Muffled thuds came from inside Hadi's room. Something wasn't right. Babauta raised his M4 and opened the door. Saffa tackled the sergeant as he entered, thrusting the blade deep into Babauta's shoulder. The soldier roared with anger and pain. Both men clawed, bit, gouged, and kicked with all their might.

In spite of his wound, Babauta held his own, landing several savage blows.

Saffa knew the big American would overpower him if this lasted much longer. He had to end it quickly. He stunned Babauta with a well-timed chop to the throat, then raised his blade for the killing strike. Babauta fired his M4, sending a bullet through Saffa's thigh. The colonel howled and buried the knife in Babauta's side.

The islander fell to the floor. Saffa grabbed Hadi and limped to his car.

*****

When the medical platoon reached the mosque, Crumm was already there. He wore sunglasses to cover his swollen black eye.

Stuart approached the captain. "What happened?"

"Car bomb. There was another bomber inside, but his vest malfunctioned." He pointed to Hussein. "That policeman caught him."

Lieutenant Hussein sat on a cinder block smoking a cigarette. He looked shaken.

It appeared that the car bomb's only victim was the bomber himself. Parts of him were everywhere. Stuart beheld the scattered, charred shreds of what used to be a human being. Instead of nausea, he now felt sorrow at the appalling waste of life.

*****

Babauta burst into Allen's quarters and collapsed.

Allen rushed to his side. "What happened?"

Babauta was bleeding heavily from the knife wounds. "Hadi gone. Saffa taking him. I trying to stop him. I'm sorry." The sergeant's eyes rolled back in his head as he lost consciousness.

Allen cradled him in his arms and yelled, "MEDIC! MEDIC!"

26

Saffa stuffed Hadi in his Dodge Durango, which was purchased with American taxpayer dollars, and snarled, "You speak, you die." He then grabbed an undershirt from a laundry bag and bandaged his bloody leg.

The base was on high alert. News of the bomb in Tuz and a soldier stabbed on Bernstein had spread like wildfire. Soldiers darted everywhere in full battle gear. No one stopped Saffa, but he knew he had to get out fast. There was no time to go through the Iraqi side of the base. He made a break for the north gate. The confused guards jumped aside as he blew past. They were prepared to stop people from breaking in, but not out.

*****

Allen left the medical bunker in a daze. He was covered in Babauta's blood. He stumbled to the command bunker, threw open the door and shouted, "Get a chopper now! Saffa just stabbed Babauta and kidnapped Hadi. Get a patrol together. I know where he's headed."

The officer on duty scrambled his team. "You got it. Give us a minute."

Allen turned to go. "I'll get my gear."

*****

The medical platoon was still at the mosque. Stuart stood next to his Humvee while Vasquez pulled security from the gunner's hatch.

A mob was gathering. Arabs filled the street, chanting angrily. They pumped their fists in the air and shouted anti-Kurdish mantras. Rumors quickly spread that the attack was retaliation against the Arabs for the Kurds killed by the car bomb days before. Simmering racial tensions threatened to flash into an inferno of hate and death.

Lieutenant Hussein gathered his men and tried to disperse the crowd.

Stuart and Vasquez watched Hussein's men wrestle the ringleaders to the ground. Stuart said, "This is getting ugly."

The vehicle's radio erupted with urgent traffic. Vasquez ducked into the cabin to hear the chatter. "Shit!"

Stuart asked, "What is it?"

"Colonel Saffa just stabbed Sergeant Babauta and took off with Hadi! Captain Allen's putting together a mission to stop him!"

"How badly is Babauta hurt?"

"Didn't say."

*****

Allen returned to the command center with his gear. "Where's my patrol?"

The officer on duty replied sullenly, "It's been canceled."

"Who gave the order?"

"I did." Colonel Thorne stepped from his office.

"But Saffa has Hadi! He's gonna kill him!"

"Get back to your quarters. That's an order!"

"No."

"Get back to your bunk or I'll have you thrown in the detention center."

"Go to hell!"

"At ease, Captain!"

Allen's fist careened into Thorne's face. The colonel went down.

Allen left his commander sprawled on the floor. Outside, he found the ghostly forms of Buck, Stubb, and Flask waiting for him. One of them pointed to Thorne's Humvee parked nearby – an M240 mounted in its turret.

*****

Vasquez called to Stuart, "Captain Allen just decked Thorne, stole his Humvee, and took off on his own to save Hadi! He's calling on the radio for help! Thorne's ordered everybody to arrest him!"

Stuart ran to Crumm. "Hadi's been kidnapped. Captain Allen is trying to rescue him all by himself. We've got to help."

Crumm snorted. "Not my problem."

"A child will be murdered if we don't help. He doesn't have much time."

"I already warned you about Allen. Calm down before you end up like him." Crumm walked away.

Stuart cursed under his breath, then spotted Lieutenant Hussein. The young police officer and his men were nearly finished dispersing the angry crowd. Stuart ran to him. "Lieutenant Hussein! Captain Allen's in trouble! I need your help!"

Seconds later, Stuart sat in the back of Hussein's squad car. The lieutenant sat in the passenger seat. The driver started to pull out when one of the doors opened. Vasquez piled into the back seat with Stuart and said, "I'm going too."

The car sped north in a cloud of dust toward the hills outside of town.

*****

Near the cave, Saffa heard on the radio that Allen was mounting a mission to hunt him down. He grabbed the hand mic and called his headquarters. "An American officer is trying to kill me! He is mad! Get a platoon to my location now! Here are the coordinates…"

He grabbed Hadi and limped into the cavern. "Now you will show me your secret!"

*****

Allen spotted Saffa's vehicle near the cave and dismounted. He grabbed some chem-lights and ran to the entrance. Once there, he grabbed the flashlight from his armored vest and put on the infrared lens. Allen snapped one of the chem-lights, threw it into the cavern, and donned his night vision goggles. Flashlight in one hand and pistol in the other, he crawled through the hole.

The cavern was still pitch black, but, through Allen's goggles, the chem-light glowed like a campfire in the floor. He heard shouts from deep in the cave and picked up his pace.

Allen's night vision spotted the faint glow of a lit match in the tunnel ahead. He broke another glow stick and silently placed it on the ground as he advanced, M9 pistol at the ready.

The goggles allowed Allen to see in the dark, but cut off his peripheral vision. His helmet banged loudly against the same outcropping Faisal had hit his head on. The thud echoed through the cave. Allen froze.

Saffa grabbed Hadi and raised his pistol. A bullet careened down the tunnel, sparking brightly as it ricocheted past Allen.

Allen called to Saffa, "Let the boy go!"

The reply came quickly. Another bullet bounced past Allen. Saffa's voice reverberated in its wake. "Come get him!" He fired again.

In the muzzle flashes, Hadi spotted the bloody wound on Saffa's thigh. He punched it as hard as he could. Saffa yelped and released his grasp.

Allen saw a form running at him. He raised his pistol then lowered it. "Hadi! It's me, Captain Allen!"

*****

A phone call had summoned Colonel Hagir to the cliffs overlooking Hadi's cave. The Kurdish police chief watched the events unfold from his perch. Three Iraqi Army trucks ground to a halt outside the entrance. Troops piled out and dispersed.

Colonel Hagir lowered his binoculars and sighed. "Captain Allen is doomed."

*****

After a few more miles, Hussein's car came upon a group of Iraqi soldiers outside the cave. Stuart spotted Thorne's Humvee nearby. "They're here!" He jumped out and scrambled toward the cave entrance. Vasquez ran to the Humvee to try the radio. Hussein and his driver stayed with the squad car.

An Iraqi Army captain approached Hussein. "You're out of your jurisdiction."

Hussein asked, "Where is Saffa?"

"Why do you want to know?"

"The Americans said he stabbed one of their men and ran off with a local boy."

"That's true." He raised his pistol and shot Hussein twice in the chest.

Hussein flew back, limp, onto the rocky ground.

The captain turned the weapon on Hussein's driver. The young policeman's head rocked violently in a halo of red mist. He stared at his killer for a second as if confused then fell to the ground – his dead eyes still staring in disbelief.

The Iraqi captain wiped the spattered gore from his face and walked toward the cave.

27

Stuart called to Allen from the mouth of the cave, "Captain Allen! Are you in there?"

"Yeah! I've got Hadi! He's okay! I'll send him to you!" He pushed the boy toward the exit. "Go! Get outta here!"

The boy scurried toward Stuart.

Stuart yelled, "Come on! We've got Hadi! Let's get out of here!"

Allen replied, "I'm going to finish this!" He watched Hadi to make sure the boy got out. As he turned back toward the gloom, Saffa smashed a rock into the side of his head.

*****

Colonel Hagir watched Saffa's men shoot Hussein and his driver. He cursed and slammed his fist on the hood of his squad car.

His cell phone rang. Hagir pulled it from his pocket and checked the number. It was the same one that brought him here.

Al-Khayal.

*****

Allen hit the ground, dropping his M9. His helmet took the brunt of the rock's impact, but his goggles were smashed.

Saffa put his pistol to Allen's chest. The flash lit the cave like a strobe light, but the captain was unharmed. The bullet embedded harmlessly in his armor.

Saffa aimed at Allen's face and pulled the trigger again. *Click.* The gun was empty. Allen swept the colonel's feet, sending him to the ground hard.

The two fought tooth and nail in the blackness. Only one could leave alive.

*****

Hadi made it to Stuart. The professor hugged the boy. "Let's get help." They started for the Humvee.

A shot rang out. A bullet hit the rock inches from Hadi's head. Stuart jerked the boy back behind a boulder.

Peeking around the rock, Stuart counted at least ten Iraqi soldiers closing in fast.

*****

Crumm's men were finishing up at the mosque when his cell phone rang. It was Thorne. The colonel said, "It's time to deal with Allen once and for all. Go alone to these coordinates immediately…"

*****

Saffa put Allen in a sleeper hold. The Iraqi's powerful arms cut the blood flow to the American's brain.

Allen felt himself blacking out. His strength ebbed as he tried to break Saffa's vice grip. A voice whispered to him from the growing miasma in his mind. It told him what to do.

With the last of his might, Allen pulled Babauta's knife from its sheath and thrust it deep into the Iraqi's wounded leg. Saffa yelped, and released his hold. Allen gasped for air, trying to regain his senses.

Saffa clutched the knife and pulled it free with a cry of rage. Allen pounced before the Iraqi could bring the blade to bear. The men battled savagely for the weapon. In the struggle, it tumbled into the darkness.

Saffa kicked with his good leg. His foot found Allen's fake limb. The prosthetic cracked. The American hit the ground.

Allen played the last card he had. He jerked off his helmet and swung it as hard as he could. A hollow crack told him he'd found his target.

Saffa went limp. He was out cold.

Allen heard Stuart calling to him. "It's a trap! We're being shot at!"

Rifle reports echoed into the cave. Allen groped the gritty floor and found his pistol. With gritted teeth, he put the M9 to the unconscious colonel's head. "No." He lowered the weapon. "I won't let you make me a murderer." He yelled to Stuart, "On my way!" Allen grabbed Saffa's empty pistol, loaded a fresh magazine, and hobbled to the entrance.

*****

Stuart huddled behind the boulder with Hadi, shielding the boy with his body. The Iraqi soldiers were nearly upon them. One appeared and aimed his rifle at Stuart with a smile. Stuart closed his eyes and held Hadi tight.

He heard the shot, but felt no pain. He looked up to see the Iraqi falling backward with half his face missing. Allen's head and arm protruded from the cave. The captain swung the pistol and quickly shot two more attackers.

The sudden deaths of three of their number gave the Iraqis pause. Stuart and Hadi pulled Allen behind the boulder. The captain gave Saffa's pistol to the teacher. "Here, it's ready to go. Make every shot count."

Stuart took the weapon with trepidation. "But you said-"

"Yeah. We're fucked."

The shooting started again with deafening intensity. Allen raised his pistol. "Here they come!"

A new sound echoed through the hills. It was the rapid staccato of a machine gun. Stuart looked to his left. Tracers flew in his direction. He instinctively took cover, then realized the fire wasn't aimed at him. He peered over the boulder to see Vasquez manning the M240 atop Thorne's Humvee.

More Iraqis went down as the young soldier operated the weapon with deadly efficiency. Most of the surviving Iraqis retreated under the withering storm of lead, but some diehards took cover in the rocks and returned fire.

*****

The Iraqi army captain, his face still smeared with the policeman's blood, approached Thorne's Humvee from the rear. He was unseen by

Vasquez, who continued to pour fire into Saffa's men from the Humvee's gun turret.

The Iraqi's pistol was useless against the American's helmet and body armor, but this dragon's tough hide had a weakness. It offered no protection on the sides. The traitor crept to Vasquez's flank. He aimed his pistol carefully. It was time to slay this fire-belching beast.

Three shots rang out. Vasquez heard the pops and turned to see the Iraqi turncoat collapse. Hussein stood behind the fallen attacker, his pistol still smoking in his hand.

Hussein fell to his knees, grabbing his side. His ribs were broken, but his Kevlar vest had saved his life.

*****

Hagir's face was grim as he spoke to his master, "No. You go too far. I cannot do it."

"I know you are fond of Captain Allen. Do not let this cloud your judgment. He has ruined too many of our plans. He must be eliminated for the cause...For Kurdistan."

"What about Saffa?"

"The Arab fool's greed has made him a liability. His usefulness is at an end."

"But-"

"Now do as I say."

"Yes...It will be done." He hung up and hesitated, trying to justify what he was about to do. "For Kurdistan." He dialed another number. "Hello, Colonel Thorne. I need your help."

*****

Thorne came running into the command center, his jaw sporting a knot the size of a baseball. "Fire mission! We've got an urgent fire mission for the artillery!"

The sergeant in charge of plotting the targets for the M109 howitzers rose to his feet. "Yes, sir. What are the coordinates and who's the observer?"

"Here!" Thorne gave the sergeant a grid location written on a scrap of paper. "The observer is Colonel Hagir. Rogue Iraqi soldiers are attacking his men in the hills north of Tuz."

"Sir, I can't fire that mission. We gotta have an American on the ground to confirm the coordinates. It's regulation."

"Sergeant, I am ordering you put fire on that location!" He pointed to the paper.

"I'm sorry, sir, but I can't do it." The sergeant held firm.

Thorne gritted his teeth. "Wait just a minute."

*****

Crumm pulled onto a cliff across the valley from Hagir. He spotted Allen in the firefight below and smirked. *Idiot.*

His phone rang. Thorne relayed the coordinates for the artillery strike to him. Crumm checked his map. It would come down right on Allen's head.

Crum smiled. *Poor Captain Allen.*

"I confirm that grid. Multiple hostiles in the open. Request immediate suppression."

28

The artillery was inbound.

Hagir called Al-Khayal. "It is done." He lowered the phone with a sigh. "Insha Allah."

*****

Al-Khayal was satisfied. That was one less trail that could lead back to him. He would soon eliminate another. Al-Khayal always covered his tracks well. The hajji shop would mysteriously close after today. He would shed this identity like a snake's discarded skin to melt into the shadows.

A voice called from behind him, "Hey, Ed! What's good today?"

Ayad smiled and pocketed his cell phone. He turned to greet a group of American soldiers as they entered his shop. "Hello, my friends! Sit down! Would you like some chai?"

*****

Vasquez kept the Iraqis pinned down mercilessly. Allen saw his chance. He tossed two hand grenades at the attackers. Then he, Stuart, and Hadi made a break for the Humvee.

Allen fell. His broken prosthetic wouldn't support him. He scrambled desperately on his hands and knees – bullets impacting around him. He watched Stuart and Hadi run for the Humvee. They were almost there. Allen knew he didn't have a chance, so he stopped and covered them with his M9.

*****

Saffa plodded on his elbows toward the cave entrance. His wounded leg trailed limply behind him. He lit his way with a pack of matches from his pocket. He was bleeding and exhausted, but his anger propelled him.

*****

Stuart saw Allen and turned back. Hadi tried to follow.

Stuart grabbed the boy and pointed to the Humvee. "Go! Imshi!" Hadi understood. He dashed to the vehicle and got inside. Once the boy was safe, Stuart sprinted to Allen.

The captain waved him off. "Get outta here!"

"Bullshit! You're coming with me!"

Stuart dragged Allen by his body armor. A bullet hit Stuart's thigh. He hit the ground, grabbing his leg. He saw bone jutting from the grisly wound, but felt no pain. Everything happened in slow motion. It was the Speicher mess hall again, but this time it was *his* blood flowing.

A crackling sound filled the air. Allen yelled, "INCOMING!" and climbed on top of the dazed professor to shield him with is body.

High explosive rounds rained down, not caring who they killed.

Vasquez dropped into the Humvee and tried to call for help. It was no use. The hills blocked the signal.

Shrapnel peppered the side of the Humvee.

A round struck the mountainside above the cave entrance. The mouth vomited a geyser of dust and debris as it collapsed.

*****

Saffa made his way to the cavern just as hell arrived. In an instant, the roof imploded with such force, he was blown back into the tunnel.

When the deafening noise finally ceased, Saffa reached into his pocket for his last remaining match. He hesitated, unsure if he wanted to see what it would reveal.

With trembling hands, Saffa lit the tiny torch. The flickering luminescence revealed what he had feared. The entire cavern was caved in. He was trapped.

He glanced at the tunnel wall and saw an image. It was a mustached warrior with a wounded leg. As the little flame faded, Saffa found the next image. It was of a jet-black bull with massive wings and a lion's head devouring the wounded warrior.

The match flickered out, plunging Saffa into darkness. He heard movement from deep in the cave. "Who is there?" The rustling was closer now. "Stay away from me!" His voice rebounded back to him from every direction. Then he heard it again. It was right on top of him. "STAY AWAY!" Before the echo died, it was replaced by blood curdling screams reverberating in the abyss.

*****

The artillery barrage persisted. Allen still covered Stuart. Shrapnel pelted Allen's armor and helmet. A piece found his side, knocking the breath from him. He rolled off of Stuart, gasping for breath.

"Come on!" Stuart tugged Allen's vest.

They struggled together across the open ground. They finally reached the Humvee and climbed in. Stuart noticed Lieutenant Hussein in the back seat. Wearily, he nodded his thanks to the policeman.

Vasquez jumped into the driver's seat, started the engine and sped toward the highway. A shell impacted next to the Humvee. The vehicle nearly flipped.

Every window was cracked, there were holes in the hood, the engine was smoking, the right rear tire was shredded, the radio antenna was blown off, and blood was smeared all over the interior. But the Humvee still ran.

Stuart was pale and barely conscious. Allen pointed at the professor's leg. "We gotta get a tourniquet on that." He removed his belt and wrapped it tightly around Stuart's thigh. Allen coughed. Blood dribbled from his mouth onto his vest. The heavy ceramic plate of his body armor pressed on his chest, making it hard to breathe. He undid the Velcro fastener to get some air.

*****

Vasquez didn't stop at the gate when he got to Bernstein. He laid on the horn and waved the guards aside, yelling, "We got wounded! Call for the choppers!" Once past the gate, he raced to the medical bunker.

Allen was pale again. He leaned toward Stuart and said, "Promise me you'll tell them."

"Tell who?" Stuart was barely conscious.

Allen clutched Stuart's collar. "Promise me!"

"Okay…I'll tell them. I promise."

"Don't let it take you, Doc." The captain pulled Stuart closer. "Don't let this place take you too."

Allen released his grip and let out a long, gurgling breath. The captain was dead.

The battalion surgeon and his team were waiting when they pulled up. Hussein and Vasquez helped put Allen and Stuart onto stretchers.

Vasquez walked to the command bunker and shoved the soldier keeping the unit log aside. He pulled the flash drive from his pocket and started copying files.

*****

Hussein was treated by the medics and released late that afternoon. He walked with Hadi to the front gate to meet the police cars that would take them back to Tuz. Silhouetted against the setting desert sun, the Kurdish boy reached up and grasped the Arab policeman's hand.

Hussein said in Arabic. "It is time for you to go home."

Hadi didn't understand his words, but he knew what the policeman said.

*****

The medics rushed Allen and Stuart into the bunker. Stuart saw Babauta lying unconscious on the surgeon's table. The islander was covered in blood.

The Blackhawk arrived quickly. Had it not already been en route for Babauta, Stuart would have lost his leg.

Stuart awakened momentarily on the chopper and saw the flight crew working desperately over Babauta, who lay next to him.

"We're losing him!" he heard one of them call out.

He felt someone watching him. He looked between the pilots. He could see nothing, but he knew someone…something was there. Hovering. Watching. Waiting.

The aircraft lurched. Stuart's head spun with vertigo. He reached for the sergeant's hand and squeezed it before blacking out.

*****

Stuart's next lucid moment was in the military hospital in Balad. He was in a bed. It was nighttime. The lights were turned down low. His leg was heavily bandaged and hurt like hell, but Stuart was thankful to still have it.

He flagged down a passing nurse. "Can you please tell me the condition of Sergeant Babauta? We flew in on the same chopper."

The nurse sighed. "I'm sorry. The sergeant didn't make it. He went into arrest while the chopper was in the air. He was dead on arrival. There was nothing we could do."

*****

Crumm and Thorne met privately in the colonel's quarters. Crumm was coming unhinged. "What am I going to do? There's no way out of this one! Vasquez and the egghead weren't supposed to survive. I confirmed the artillery that killed Allen. It's in the log. They can corroborate it."

Thorne held up a hand. "Calm down. There's always a way out. You just have to look in the right place." He took a sip of whiskey. "The log is kept on a computer, right? With a little editing, Allen will be the one that called in the big guns…right on his own head."

"That might work."

Thorne refilled Crumm's drink. "Of course it will. You're smart. That's why I brought you into our arrangement with the Al-Khayal. We stay out of his business and he takes care of us. Allen was too strong headed. He was a problem."

Crumm took a swig. "You're sure it won't lead back to me?"

Thorne gave a sly grin, "Just keep your cool and we'll both go home war heroes. I'm recommending you for the Silver Star."

Crumm smiled.

Thorne held up a silk rug. "We'll go home wealthy men thanks to our side ventures." He took another sip of whiskey, pausing to enjoy the flavor. "As long as we play our parts, everything'll be just fine." He smiled. "I've got your back. Trust me."

*****

Vasquez met Crumm's supply sergeant late that night. The sergeant handed him a thick manila envelope. "I hope you know what you're doin'."

Vasquez stuffed the package under his shirt. "So do I."

THE DEVIL'S DUE

The Evening News
Two Months Later

"And now back to our reporter on the ground in Baghdad."

"Thanks, Chip. A case is unfolding here in Iraq that has many casting accusations of corruption and conspiracy. Captain Lester Crumm is being held in an undisclosed location here in Iraq. He faces charges including dereliction of duty, drug trafficking, accepting bribes, falsifying records, conspiring with insurgents, and murder to name a few. The most serious charges center around the role he played in the deaths of several American soldiers.

"His commanding officer, Lieutenant Colonel Bruce Thorne, had this to say:"

A video clip of Thorne at a press conference filled the screen. "I hope the charges against this officer prove to be false. But let me assure you...If he is found guilty, he will be punished to the fullest extent of military law."

The reporter's face returned. "You'll remember we were the first to break this story after an anonymous manila envelope arrived in our news office. It contained documents providing evidence of Crumm's alleged offenses.

"New allegations are surfacing daily. Some are saying that this case won't stop with Captain Crumm. This could turn out to be just the tip of an iceberg whose scale we can only imagine."

*****

Military Detention Facility
Somewhere in Iraq

Thorne walked into a room containing a small table and two folding chairs. He was there to visit his former protégé. He took a seat.

191

Crumm entered in shackles and sat opposite him. A guard stood watch in the corner.

"How are they treating you?" Thorne forced a smile.

Crumm sneered, "Like a criminal."

"I brought this for you." Thorne held out a rolled up black beret.

The guard stepped forward. Thorne said calmly, "It's just his beret. Captain Crumm will need to wear it in court. This one's already broken in. You know how hard it is to get a new one to look right."

The guard stepped back.

Thorne whispered to Crumm, "Use it soon."

Crumm unrolled the beret. A razorblade was tucked in the fold. "What the hell is this?"

"I'm sorry it has to be this way. We can't let you go on trial."

Crumm gritted his teeth, "I'll rat you all out."

Thorne shook his head. "You won't get the chance. You'll never make it to trial." He glanced at the thin blade. "If you don't do it, the Iraqis will. It won't be quick and it won't be pretty. This is your only choice. Trust me."

Tears came to Crumm's eyes.

"I wish I could do more. I really do." Thorne rose to leave. "I'm sorry. My hands are tied."

*****

Residence of Doctor Stuart Knight
Knoxville, TN
10:30 AM
Sunday

Stuart sat in his favorite recliner – his leg propped up on a matching ottoman. A metal brace covered the wounded limb from hip to ankle.

His copy of *The Archaeology of Ancient Mesopotamia* rested on the table next to his chair. It was waiting for him in his office at the university when he returned home after weeks of rehab at Walter Reed Army Hospital. The book had been wrapped in a dusty brown package. The return address was simply an APO in Iraq – no name.

He placed the tome in his lap. Fine sand impregnated the spaces between every page. Stuart opened it as he had done every day since returning home. A large rectangular hole was cut into its center. The cavity contained the black idol.

He reached into the breast pocket of his tweed blazer and withdrew three envelopes. He'd found them tucked into the book. One had Stuart's name on it. The names "Emily" and "Little Jake" were written on the other two. Stuart returned the last two letters to his pocket.

He opened his and read it again.

Doc,

If you're reading this, you made it home alive. I'm betting I didn't.

I need you to do something for me. I've included letters to my wife and son. Please deliver them. I need you to do it in person. Tell them I'm sorry. I'm sorry for letting them down.

Tell them they should have been my mission. I know that now, but it's too late.

When I took the statue, I planned to smash it and save you from ending up like me. But then I realized it's a choice you have to make. You have to destroy it or it will destroy you.

It's not too late for you. Let it go, Stuart. Save yourself. Don't let this place take you too.

Jake Allen

Stuart put down the letter and stared at the idol. He reached out his hand, but withdrew just short of touching it.

He shut the book and sat in silence, thoughtfully running his fingers over the cover.

Stuart rose stiffly from his chair, limped to his bookshelf, and slid the volume into the same space it had occupied before he departed for Iraq.

He opened his wallet and pulled out the picture of his daughter, Rachel. He looked from her to the letter of resignation resting on his oak desk.

It was time for Stuart to go home. His place was with his wife and child in California. He knew that now.

He'd seen enough anger and bitterness. Stuart prayed, yes, prayed that his wife and he could find forgiveness and reconciliation. He wanted to be a family again. He'd talked with her on the phone several times. She wanted the same thing. At least he hoped she did.

Stuart checked his watch. Almost time for church. He began attending services soon after returning from Iraq. His experiences awakened him to the possibility of the existence of things unseen. Parson's premonitions, the djinn, the angel of death.

Was any of it real? Does it matter?

He once asked himself the difference between superstition and faith. Now he knew. Superstition was adhering to that which you know in your mind to be foolish. Faith was believing in that which you hope in your heart to be true. One was rooted in fear, the other in love.

Stuart hoped his new faith would give him the strength to repair his family. He also hoped it would give him the strength to carry out Allen's last request.

Stuart felt a sudden chill. He caught a shadow moving in the corner of his eye. He looked again, but saw nothing.

There are more things in heaven and earth, Horatio…

He grabbed his cane, opened the door, and shielded his face. The vibrant green Tennessee countryside hurt his eyes. They were still accustomed to the arid, desert landscape of Iraq.

Stuart had put this day off as long as he dared. He was going to Allen's home that afternoon. He would deliver the letters to his widow and try to answer the questions she would surely have.

He thought of the young son that would never know his father. Stuart's heart ached for the child. The boy was too young to know that he, like Stuart, was one of the ever growing legions destined to spend the rest of their lives haunted by the ghosts of Babylon.

Made in the USA
Charleston, SC
27 October 2012